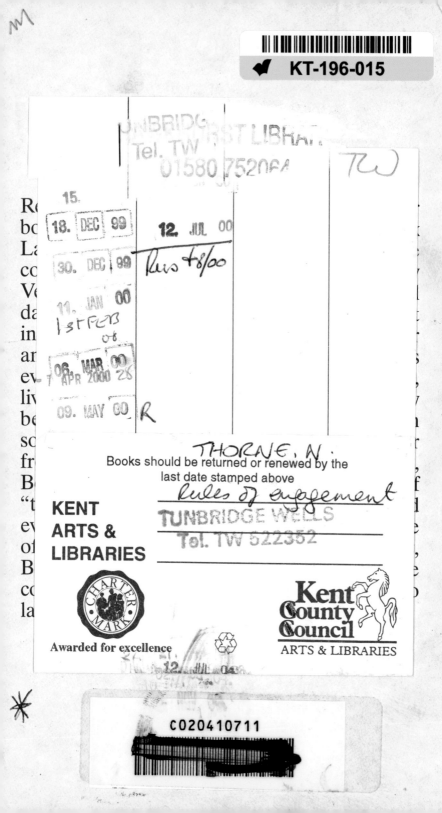

RULES OF ENGAGEMENT

Nicola Thorne

CHIVERS PRESS
BATH

First published 1997
by
Severn House Publishers
This Large Print edition published by
Chivers Press
by arrangement with
Severn House Publishers Ltd
1998

ISBN 0 7540 2095 9

British Library Cataloguing in Publication Data available

Printed and bound in Great Britain by
REDWOOD BOOKS, Trowbridge, Wiltshire

CHAPTER ONE

Becky stood at the window watching Henry Lamb as he filled the wheelbarrow with the dead leaves of autumn and, at a leisurely pace, trundled along the path to tip it on the growing pile somewhere at the bottom of the garden, just out of sight of the house.

Arms akimbo she waited until he reappeared, his barrow empty, maintaining the same steady pace along the path, pipe in mouth, with apparently all the time in the world, and oblivious of her presence.

Suddenly an arm sidled round Becky's waist and lips brushed her cheeks. Startled, she turned and saw surprise in the warm brown eyes of the man looking tenderly down at her.

'Becky?' His eyes went from her to the man with the wheelbarrow, now a few feet away from them. 'You seemed very intent on the gardener.'

'He's not the gardener.' Becky's soft voice sounded amused. 'That's Henry Lamb. We used to play together as children.'

The man beside her peered out of the window more intently. 'Henry Lamb,' he murmured. 'Well he looks *very* like the gardener to me.'

'You're a snob Max,' Becky taunted, breaking away from him, turning her back on the autumnal view from the window and the

1

sight of Henry forking up the leaves.

The expression on Max's handsome, affable face grew perplexed. 'How can you call me a snob, darling, when I refer to someone who is obviously doing something in the garden as "a gardener"?'

'He's helping out.' Becky's tone was now offhand. 'He does odd jobs for people. He's actually a writer,' she continued, as though that was the end of the matter.

'Oh a *writer*.' Max's voice was heavy with sarcasm. '*That* explains it.'

'I can't understand you, Max.' Becky's expression became one of bewilderment. 'You are normally such a kind person. This shows me a different side of you.'

'Look, darling.' Anxiously her fiancé crossed the room towards her and gently spun her round so that his eyes stared deep into hers. 'What's wrong with you? What's up?' He led her to the sofa and, after pushing her gently down, seated himself next to her. 'You seem all out of sorts today and I thought it was going to be such a happy day. Our engagement party tonight, everyone in the house in a tizz. Your mother is so excited. Yet here I see you staring broodily out of the window and when I make a remark, in all innocence, you call me a snob. Is there something between you and this fellow?' His voice sounding jocular, he jerked his head in the direction of the garden.

'Don't be silly.' Becky, apparently also

2

amused, shook her head. 'He's an old family friend. He tries to support himself by writing, and does odd jobs round the village.'

'I apologise. I realise now how awful my remarks must have sounded.' Max leaned towards her, his lips placatingly brushing her cheek.

But to his touch her flesh seemed cold, unresponsive. Becky remained staring thoughtfully at her lap in a pose he considered very unlike that of the warm, even passionate, woman he had wooed—with some difficulty at first—and finally won.

'Look Becky *is* there something?' He held out his hands. 'You're not at all your jolly old self. Not having regrets?'

'Of *course* not.' She seemed to make a determined effort to throw off her mood and attempted a smile. 'The fact is that seeing Henry did upset me a bit. I know how badly he wants to succeed and how difficult it is for him. He can't *enjoy* doing the garden when he would rather be writing; but he's got such spirit I admire him. He never complains.'

Max rose and walked to the window where, in his turn, he stood looking for the man whose presence seemed to disturb his idyll with his beloved. Only now the barrow stood empty beside a neat pile of freshly raked leaves and Henry Lamb was nowhere to be seen.

*   *   *

3

'Poor Henry,' Lady Versey exclaimed over lunch, 'one does feel so sorry for him.' She glanced in the direction of Max who was listening to her, respectfully as usual, as if his whole attention were riveted on her. He *was* a charmer, Becky's mother thought, smiling at him. Tall and very masculine with thick brown hair, and kind, intelligent eyes, he was someone who would sweep any woman off her feet.

At times in the past Becky had made her anxious the way she and Henry seemed to get together every time she was home. They had grown up by the sea and both liked sailing. Henry took her out in the small dinghy he had anchored by his fisherman's cottage at the water's edge in the bay. Henry was attractive too; but he was almost family.

Secretly, as much as they may have despised themselves for this attitude, people like the Verseys did not consider a man who was completely without fortune or prospects, as a suitable match for their only daughter. Much as they liked Henry, much as *everyone* liked him, deep down they could never have welcomed him as a son-in-law.

Thank heaven for Max, who Becky had introduced to the household about six months before. They had appeared unannounced from London, obviously deeply in love, and the whole family had taken to him—clearly with relief. Looks, charm, money—above all, position—they couldn't help regarding him as

4

an ideal match for their daughter. It appeared he was an executive in the advertising agency where Becky worked as a visualiser.

The Verseys were successful people and they felt at ease with others like themselves. Sir John Versey had been knighted for his services not only to industry but for his contribution to the party in power. He was rich, articulate and successful and he instinctively felt on equal terms with people like himself.

'Poor *Henry*,' Sir John scoffed. 'Nonsense. He has himself to blame if he earns a tenner a day sweeping up leaves. No one asked him to. He could have got a proper job like everyone else.' Sir John gazed knowingly at Max. 'We love Henry, but,' he shrugged, 'can't understand people who opt out.' He held out the decanter of wine in the direction of Max, who put a hand over his glass.

'No more, thank you, Sir John,' he said with a smile, 'I don't normally drink at midday.'

Sir John nodded approvingly and put the stopper firmly back on the decanter. 'Exactly my policy. In these days of intense competition one doesn't want to take the edge off.'

'Anyway you'll have a chance to meet Henry socially tonight.' Lady Versey glanced at a list of names at her elbow. 'Of course he'll be here for the party.'

'I hope you don't mind us inviting the *gardener*?' Becky gave Max a wicked smile and, as he looked at her, his heart turned over. She was wicked, tantalising, thrilling. Sometimes he couldn't believe his luck that she was his.

For she *was* his. They kept their own apartments in town, but the weekends were spent together. Often they stayed in bed all day, tucked up with the Sunday papers, eating a delicious brunch and watching the football match on TV in the afternoon. It was his idea of heaven.

'I'd be *most* happy to meet the gardener.' Max's slightly mocking tone suited hers. 'Meanwhile you promised to show me the beach.'

'Oh I've got to help Mummy this afternoon.' Becky glanced at Lady Versey. 'There's loads to do.'

'There's nothing for *you* to do,' her mother said firmly. 'We have a reliable firm of caterers who are doing everything. You two young people run off and enjoy yourselves but be sure you're back in time for the party.'

'And I must get back to the office.' Sir John, a youthful fifty, leapt to his feet, 'Or *I'll* be late for the party too.'

* * *

It was a blustery afternoon and towards the end, after exploring the village, the lovers clung together as they walked heads down against the strong wind blowing in from the Channel. Stone, the dog, ran after them. A beautiful

6

golden Labrador, he had been given his curious name when Becky, seeing him as a pup, had exclaimed, 'Isn't he *beautiful*? His coat's the colour of stone.' Stone was now two years old and he raced ahead, his mouth open, tongue hanging out, clearly delighted with the unexpected treat of an afternoon walk on the beach.

'I love your mother and father,' Max roared in Becky's ear against the wind.

'And they love you.'

'I'm so happy,' he shouted back.

'Me too.' Impulsively she put her arm round his waist. 'We're going to be the happiest couple in the world.'

'We are.' He looked down at her vibrant face. With her pale golden hair blowing behind her, her intense blue eyes aglow with happiness, she looked like a Viking princess. How he loved her. He remembered the day she'd come, fresh out of art school, for an interview. Even if she hadn't been able to draw a line he guessed he'd have taken her on. Then, she had been twenty-one and he twenty-seven and the creative director. That was two years ago. It had been love at first sight for him, but not for her. She proved hard to get and it wasn't until she'd been there almost a year that he'd finally taken her out.

'This Henry,' Max shouted once more against the wind screaming in their ears, 'he's not a *threat* is he?'

'Don't be absurd.' Becky pulled up and, winding her college scarf more tightly around her neck, pointed to an isolated cottage at the side of the beach. 'That's where he lives. He's a recluse, eccentric . . . how could I *possibly* prefer someone like Henry to *you*? Besides he's . . .' she paused and Max gazed curiously at her.

'Gay?' he ventured.

'Oh I don't think he's *gay*, but he's unusual . . . not like other men.'

'How was he when you were children?' They recommenced their walk, buffeted all the time by the wind, Stone now a golden speck in the distance as he tore after the cheeky gulls that alighted in flocks on the beach as though challenging him to come and get them.

'How do you mean?' She glanced at him.

'What was he like?'

'Oh, different.' Becky sounded vague and put her hands over her eyes to shield them against the strong sunlight reflecting off the sea. 'He was an only child, idolised by his parents. His father was a sea captain who was lost at sea when Henry was about eleven.'

'How dreadful.' Max squeezed her arm sympathetically.

'It was one of those freak accidents. Henry's father was the captain of a large tanker which disappeared off the coast of Africa without trace. The mystery has never been solved. The family were left not very well off, but Henry continued on at a boarding school paid for by

8

the shipping line his father had worked for. However, it affected him. During the holidays we noticed he was quieter. My family were always very fond of Henry. Daddy, who is a boat-builder, regarded us all as seafaring people and took an interest in the welfare of Henry and his mother. I think they helped a bit financially.'

'Does he *still* support him?' Max looked surprised.

'Oh no, except of course that he does odd jobs around the house and garden. He works terribly hard at his books, as yet with not much success.'

'Sounds like a loser to me,' Max muttered and then, immediately, gripping her arm added, 'sorry I said that.'

'How do you mean?' Becky looked puzzled.

'About being a gardener, that sort of thing. I suppose I am jealous.'

Becky turned sharply towards him and, firmly grasping the lapels of his coat collar, pulled him towards her.

'Goof,' she said and, her clear blue eyes full of love and understanding, she raised her lips to be kissed.

Momentarily they clung together, oblivious to the sound of the sea, the roar of the wind, the cries of the gulls as they swooped low over the water, or the impatient, demanding barking of Stone who had brought them a piece of driftwood which he lay enticingly at their feet, begging for a game.

Finally the sounds that they had temporarily obliterated obtruded upon them once again and yet for a further moment they remained locked in each other's arms, aware of a unity, a harmony that made Max's remarks about jealousy seem absurd.

'This is the happiest day of my life,' he murmured at last, gently disengaging himself from her loving clasp, 'why do I have to ruin it with jealousy? The fear of losing you? I don't know.' He gazed anxiously into her eyes, which seemed to him then a mirror of the world, of his emotions. At one moment they were laughing and provocative, at another full of understanding and compassion. She was a woman of great volatility, of great depth and profundity; of many parts. Sometimes he felt he was drowning in her. He knew that she was necessary for his happiness and the thought of losing her to another man was intolerable.

Practical now, looking calm and determined, Becky linked her arm through his as after hurling the piece of driftwood as far as they could and watching Stone scurry frantically after it, they turned their backs on the wind and began to wander along the shore towards the big house that stood on the cliffs overlooking Steethey Bay and the small fisherman's shack on the other side.

*　　*　　*

10

Steethey House had belonged to the Cloughs, the family of Lady Versey, who had been born there. It was her grandfather Hugo Clough who had started the boat-building business in the then small port of Steethey, and under her father it continued to prosper. But it was Margaret Versey's husband, John, who had been an apprentice in the boatyard when she first met him, who had really brought the business to international fame and recognition because of his skills not only as a designer but, perhaps more important in the climate of today, as a businessman. It was from her father John that Becky had got her own skills as an artist, a clever visualiser and draughtswoman, and her brother Miles his entrepreneurial skills which had made him ready to step, eventually, into his father's footsteps.

Becky had grown up in a happy and contented family as well as a wealthy and prosperous one. Yet she was never spoiled, attending the local well-run comprehensive school with her brother, and when he had gone to university to do a degree in business studies Becky went to college to study art and design.

The house had been built of stone at the end of the last century on a spectacular position almost at the edge of the cliff and, as Max and Becky, laughing and out of breath, reached the top of their private cliff path and strolled hand in hand across the lawn towards the door they saw Lady Versey waving at them from the

11

porch, an anxious look on her face.

'What is it Mummy?' Becky called in alarm.

'You've been gone *such* a long time,' Lady Versey pointed to the sun which was beginning to set over the sea on the far horizon, 'I was worried.'

'Don't you think *Max* can look after me Mummy?' Becky slyly pulled her fiancé to her side. 'And Stone.' She turned to the dog who had, with great difficulty and determination, pulled almost half a branch of a tree up the steep cliff path.

'Daddy's fussing. He got back early from the office. Twenty people for dinner and then dancing. It's a little selfish of you Becky . . .'

'Sorry Mummy. We decided to look at the village and then went for a long walk. But I *did* offer to help.'

'I didn't want help, darling, that's all taken care of. I was just worried something had happened.' The furrows from her brow having vanished, immediately she smiled. 'Just a fussy mother, Max.'

'It was selfish of us Lady Versey.' Max looked contrite too. 'It won't happen again.'

'Young people get carried away I know.' Lady Versey, her humour restored, put out her arm to usher them indoors. After all she didn't want to alienate Max. The family were so relieved that the impulsive, headstrong and much beloved only daughter had decided to marry a sensible man with prospects like Max, and not a romantic adventurer like Henry.

*   *   *

The party was mostly for young people, many of them friends of Max and Becky from London whom her parents had never met before. They had arrived in an array of smart sports cars now parked in the drive and were all staying the night either in the house or at a local hotel. They were a mixture of vaguely arty people connected with Max and Becky's world—advertising or the media, copywriters, artists, visualisers, someone from the BBC. They talked a lot, and rather loudly, but on the whole Margaret and John Versey thought them an attractive, articulate bunch far removed from the crowd who had graced their own engagement party twenty-seven years before. They had been mostly Margaret's schoolfriends, their husbands or fiancés, and John's friends from the boatyard.

John Versey had never pretended to be anything but self-made. He had been a working-class boy from Lancashire who had made good and married the boss's daughter. But it was a love match and he was not without merit—a clever, capable young man who had justified his father-in-law's tremendous faith in him. Now he wanted nothing more than happiness for his own son and daughter, and both he and Margaret had approved of

13

capable, clever Max who was so obviously head over heels in love with their daughter as well.

If there was an odd man out at the party, clearly that was Henry Lamb, whom they had invited because Henry had always come to everything, having been almost part of the family since he had been left fatherless at the age of eleven. Margaret put Henry next to her while on his other side was an unattached friend of Becky's called Ruth Vine, a copywriter who she thought might rather hit it off with Henry.

The happy couple sat next to each other in the centre of the long dining table, lit with candelabra and sparkling with silver and polished glasses in which the ruby tint of red wine glowed on the white damask cloth, an old family heirloom. It was an atmosphere of opulence and luxury and many of those seeing it for the first time were impressed; Becky, with her unassuming mews flat in Wandsworth, had never appeared to anyone to be rich.

'And what do you do?' Ruth enquired politely of Henry after there had been some general chit-chat at the beginning of the meal.

Henry rubbed his nose. 'This and that.' He paused. 'You *could* say I'd like to be a writer,' he concluded.

'*Like* to?' Ruth smiled sympathetically. 'No success then yet?'

'Not yet. They say it's a difficult time in publishing.'

'It's *always* a difficult time to get a first novel published. I'm sure if you've talent you'll succeed.'

'Henry *is* very talented,' Margaret said loyally, 'he writes lovely novels about the sea. It's just a question of time, Henry, isn't it?'

'How many novels have you written?' Ruth asked.

'I'm on my third.' Henry smiled at her ruefully.

'The others were all ...' Ruth's question trailed off.

'Rejected. I go on trying.'

'That's the spirit,' Ruth said and then, as if struck by a thought, 'of course I don't know how good they are, and I couldn't possibly *promise* anything, but I have a friend who is an agent. Do you have an agent?'

Henry shook his head. 'I send them straight to the publisher.'

'I'm sure she'd give you an honest opinion and then you would have some idea of whether it was worth your while to continue.'

'Oh I'll continue,' Henry said grimly. 'Until I bust.'

'I suppose you've known Max and Becky for ages?'

'Not Max, just Becky.'

'Oh you're not a friend of both?' Ruth looked surprised as Henry shook his head.

'I'm a local man, born here. I've known Becky and Miles since we were all children.'

'Henry's like one of the family,' Margaret said breezily. 'Aren't you Henry?'

'I suppose so.' But Henry looked gloomy.

That was certainly not the way he would like to be regarded by Becky.

*   *   *

'Dance?' Henry had waited on the edge of the crowd surrounding Becky when they gathered in the drawing room after dinner, where the carpet had been taken up and the polished floor gleamed invitingly.

Reluctantly Max laughed and graciously gave way, pointing in the direction of his fiancée. 'She's all yours,' he said magnanimously.

'Thank you.' Becky smiled from one to the other, yet was conscious of an air of tension between the two men, vividly reminding her of Max's remarks earlier in the day.

She was aware too that Henry had ignored her for most of the evening, his attention evidently taken by Ruth, to whom Max had now politely turned. Easily Becky swept on to the dance floor in the arms of her partner who immediately tripped over her foot.

'Sorry,' he said smiling awkwardly. 'You know I'm not much of a dancer.' His arm tightened round her waist.

'How do you like Ruth?' Becky enquired casually.

'She seems okay.'

'I thought you'd like her.'

'Did you?' His arm tightened even more and she was aware of the intensity of the expression in his eyes as he gazed down at her, and suddenly she realised she was shocked by it. Henry was well over six feet and had the build of a rugger fullback, a position he played in a game at which he excelled as captain of the Steethey Dynamos. He had a mass of black hair without a parting, and steely blue eyes which he had inherited from his seafaring father. Becky knew that women found him attractive and she was aware now of Ruth gazing rather anxiously over Max's shoulder at them.

Ruth need not have worried. Becky never thought of Henry as anything else than a brother; a boy, then a man, she had known all her life.

Why, then, was he glowering at her now as if full of suppressed anger?

'You don't seem awfully happy,' she said, groaning inwardly as he once again trod on her foot.

'Sorry.'

'That's okay.' She flashed him a forgiving smile. 'You look as though you've got something on your mind Henry. Another rejection?'

'Yes.' He continued to gaze into her eyes, his hand clasped hers tightly.

'Oh dear. I'm sorry. Ruth told me she knew

an agent . . .'

'That's not the sort of rejection I mean,' Henry said, and in his eyes now she saw not only sadness but torment as well.

As the music died down he leaned towards her and whispered urgently, 'How could you *possibly* love someone like that?'

'Someone like *what*?' she riposted angrily, looking over her shoulder.

'Someone so smooth, so artificial, so . . .' As he raised his eyes she could see the stiff, unyielding line of his jaw, 'So unworthy of you in every way.'

At that moment the music started up again and Max, politely delivering Ruth back to Henry, took his fiancée's arm.

'I think the next dance is ours darling,' he murmured possessively in her ear, '*and* all the ones after that . . . for tonight and for the rest of our lives.'

And then very firmly and obviously he turned his back on Henry, tucked his partner's hand in his and placed his cheek against hers.

CHAPTER TWO

As her firm bold strokes swept deftly over the canvas, expertly capturing the scene in front of her, Becky found herself wondering how many times she had painted that scene of the village tucked in a cleft in the cliff and stretching eventually down to the sound and the beach, with the tiny row of coastguards' cottages at the end. Out of sight were the clusters of boats fastened at their moorings and, at the head of the estuary, the Versey boatyard, only one of many scattered at resorts on the south coast. They built yachts for an increasing army of people who, in an age of leisure, had taken to sailing as a form of sport. But a newer, and more profitable, line was the construction of powerboats which appealed to the more affluent, younger element to whom speed and its thrills was everything.

Becky stepped back and gazed critically at her canvas. Max was powerboat, Henry definitely sail. Funny how one could categorise people in this way. Max wouldn't have the time for the fiddly, pernickety process of rigging which could take up to half an hour on a blustery day ensuring that the jib, the mainsail, and the many sheets (or ropes) which secured vital parts of the boat were in place. Henry seemed to find this slow, painstaking, repetitive process fascinating. He knew all the correct procedures: how to curl the sheets about one's hand and tuck them into place and, of course, he was an expert sailor in whom instinct and experience were nicely balanced.

But it would be too slow for Max, to whom speed was a way of life. He was exciting, vitalising. He did everything in a hurry. Max would jump into a boat, start the engine, grab

19

the wheel and be off across the bay, his hair flying in the wind, his lean, handsome face alert with anticipation.

Just then her eyes were caught by a movement in the garden below as Henry rounded the side of the house with the wheelbarrow piled high with leaves, pipe stuck in the corner of his mouth, his shock of black hair looking like a coxcomb. Odd that slow old Henry should trundle past just as she was thinking of Max. He wore his customary navy nautical sweater and jeans, black fisherman's boots with the socks rolled over at the top. He looked today just as he had a week before on the day of the engagement party.

In a way she wished that time could go backwards so that the things that had happened on that day and in the course of the evening could, as it were, be replayed, could happen all over again, only with a different outcome.

For it was only that evening that she realised that Henry's feelings for her went beyond that of a mere childhood friend.

A tap on the door broke her reverie and her mother called softly, 'Coffee darling?' before quietly turning the handle.

Becky, glad of the break, put down her brush and went to open the door for her mother, who had two cups and a plate of biscuits carefully balanced on a tray. Becky smiled with pleasure. Her mother loved company and, although not

20

liking to intrude upon her daughter's work, loved to share coffee and meal breaks with her. It was so rarely that she had her to herself.

Becky took the tray from her mother and placed it on a table near her easel while Lady Versey drew up two chairs so that they could look out of the large studio window with its breathtaking view of the bay.

Becky had always loved painting and had shown talent for it at a very early age. She used to paint in one of the downstairs rooms or in her bedroom on the other side of the house and then, as a surprise for her eighteenth birthday following her success at A levels and admission to art college, her father had the attic of the house opened up for her, created a huge window in the sloping roof and presented her with the key to the studio, her very own den where no one else was admitted except with permission. And here whenever she came home, she painted, seizing the opportunity for a few hours alone crammed into the busy schedule of her life.

'May I look?' Her mother knew how secretive Becky was about her work and was delighted when her daughter nodded.

'It's nearly finished.'

Lady Versey of course had seen the view dozens of times, in reality and on canvas. This time she stood looking at it for several seconds and then exhaled deeply.

'It *is* lovely, Becky. So full of feeling. I think

21

it is the best one you've done.'

She sat down in the chair beside her daughter and began stirring her coffee.

'Why so sad darling? It's a lovely painting. Do you miss Max?'

Becky shook her head, then nodded vigorously. 'Yes. I mean, no. I mean I do miss Max and I'm not sad. Life has been so hectic recently, Mummy. I feel I hardly ever have time to myself. I so miss my weekends at home, time in my studio. All that's gone now.'

'But darling it hasn't gone.' Looking perturbed Margaret reached out for her daughter's hand. 'You *are* sad, Becky. I knew you were. Tell me darling—you are . . . happy about Max?' She looked searchingly into her daughter's eyes but their expression told her very little.

'Of course I'm happy, Mummy! What a question. I *adore* Max.'

'And he adores you,' her mother said loyally. 'I never saw such a besotted man in my life. And since he's been away he rings you every day. I think you're very lucky, darling.'

'I do too.' Becky again nodded vigorously, realising that neither she nor her mother were really addressing the question.

'It's my freedom,' she said at last.

'Your *freedom*?' Margaret Versey finished her coffee and replaced the cup on the tray.

'Since we've been engaged, every day, every minute, is taken up with Max. We work

22

together, we eat and go out together, weekends . . .'

'You could come down here at weekends,' her mother said. Even though she knew how it was with the youth of today, and there was precious little anyone could do about it, she didn't quite approve of the way her daughter and her fiancé made no secret of their sexual relationship. To a person of her generation it still took some getting used to, but one was, as it were, swept along by changing times and there could be no turning the clock back.

'Even if we *did* Max would want to be doing things all the time. He's very restless Mummy.' Becky sat back and smiled. 'It's part of his charm. One wouldn't want someone like . . .' her eyes strayed to the grounds below, but now there was no sign of him, 'Henry.'

'Oh of *course* one wouldn't want someone like Henry,' her mother expostulated and then, hastily, 'much as we love him. And one *does* love Henry.' She folded her hands on her lap. 'Nothing seems to worry him or disturb the even keel of his days. He comes at nine in the morning and leaves at one. I suppose in the afternoon he writes.'

'I suppose he does.' Becky nodded. 'I wish he *would* be successful,' she said, and added impulsively, 'I feel he so deserves it. He can't really like doing odd jobs as a handyman Mummy.'

'Oh I think he quite likes it. He has no

23

ambition you know.' She turned to her daughter. 'Not like you; not like Max. I'm so glad darling.' Momentarily an expression of anxiety passed over her mother's face. 'Well you never did care for Henry did you, not in the way . . .'

'Of *course* not, not in the way I care for Max.' Becky paused and then said, 'but I am terribly fond of him and it would make me very happy if he could be successful.'

She rose restlessly to her feet and, putting down her cup, wandered over to the window where she stood gazing down into the grounds just as, as if on cue, Henry rounded the house trundling the empty wheelbarrow. Then he paused to relight his pipe and, raising his eyes, saw her.

But he gave no sign that he had done so and bent his head again to the light of the match until it flickered and went out.

*   *   *

That afternoon as the clouds gathered in the sky promising a storm, Becky decided the light was not good enough to continue her work and, secretly to her relief, abandoned it. She ran down the stairs calling for Stone, who appeared as if from nowhere, barking with anticipation.

'Goodness what a noise!' her mother cried, emerging from the living room where she had probably been having a brief doze over the paper. She and Becky had lunched in the kitchen as usual and then had gone their separate ways, Becky back to the studio, Margaret to the living room.

'I thought I'd take a walk.' Becky emerged from the cloakroom in her thick anorak and green wellies, with the dog's lead in her hand. 'The light has gone and there may be a storm later.'

'Would you like me to come with you darling?'

'Not necessary Mummy, you go back to sleep.'

'I know you want to be alone.' Her mother touched her elbow. 'Something's bothering you, isn't it Becky? You're having a difficult time?'

'Of course I'm not!' Becky protested. 'I'm happy, I'm in love.' Then her face suddenly became serious.

'But it's a difficult time in the sense that one has to change one's life. I suppose I've been selfish, thought always of myself. Now I have someone else to think about, to put first if you like. What does Max want to do, would Max like this, that or something else ... not always what *I* might want to do at the time.'

'Does he *always* have his own way?' Margaret's expression was guarded.

'Of course he doesn't! He's incredibly generous. He wanted me to go to New York on this trip with him, at his expense.'

25

'Then why didn't you? It seems strange not to seize such an opportunity. I mean, you can always come home; you can't always go to New York.'

Becky bent down to stroke the head of Stone who was impatiently pawing the floor.

All in all it seemed that even her mother, her best friend, didn't understand.

*   *   *

By the time she got to the beach the storm clouds had disappeared and the sky in the late afternoon was of a deep, almost Mediterranean, blue. The great expanse of the sea stretched towards the horizon and, except for the cries of the gulls, the earth seemed almost unnaturally still and quiet. Becky had taken a ball for Stone which she threw vigorously towards the water and then stood, delighting in watching him scamper in. His favourite game was pretending to lose the ball, finding it and then rushing towards her with it in his mouth before laying it at her feet, and giving himself a good shake to cover her with water while she backed away laughing, before the time-honoured ritual was begun all over again.

'Oh Stone I love you,' she said falling to her knees and taking the dog's head between her hands. Then, suddenly, to her amazement she found her eyes were wet with tears and before she knew what had happened or could stop herself she was possessed by great heartfelt sobs which shook her frame and caused Stone, not normally a very perceptive dog, to stare at her in concern.

'Stone!' she cried, clasping the dog's head as she sat on the beach, her legs spread out before her, 'I am *not* very happy. It's true and I don't know why.'

Stone licked her cheek, gazed into her eyes and Becky saw, or thought she saw, a smile of sympathy and understanding such as only a well-loved pet who understood its owner could give. Despite her absences Stone was her dog and remained hers.

After a while Becky felt better, as though the release of tears had proved cathartic. After all she was young, she was loved and in love, she had loving parents, a loving dog and a perfect home. She had her health, the scenery around her was beautiful. What nonsense it was to give vent to tears on a day, at a time, like this!

She pulled out her handkerchief and gave her nose a vigorous blow and Stone, as if sensing the change, opened his mouth in what looked like a laugh and began to jump up and down again for the ball.

Becky turned and, throwing it as far as she could, watched the dog bound away after it. Then she started to run after him and the sadness was replaced by a feeling of exhilaration and, gradually, of peace.

And so eventually they came to the row of coastguard cottages at the end of the beach, much further along than the private path which led up to her house. She didn't know whether she had passed it consciously or subconsciously. She didn't know whether she really wanted to see Henry and talk to him, or whether she wished to avoid him. She seemed like a creature tossed this way and that by the wind.

Anyway his house seemed empty. He was not at home. Usually he left the door half open when he was. Often one would see him sitting in front of the door with his pipe in his mouth, hands behind his head in an attitude of relaxation; but not today.

She knew then that she had really wanted to see him, but she didn't know why. Calling to Stone she rounded the cottages along the path that led past the estuary, with the boats of various kinds moored to the buoys that floated on the water or to rings fastened in the wall at the water's edge. Ahead of her was the collection of large sheds that marked the original boatyard started by her grandfather who was a master mariner, as Henry's father had been. Only Cloughs and then Verseys had gone on to success and to fortune whereas Anthony Lamb had died at sea lost with all hands, leaving but a widow and a young son.

And that son she now saw sitting in his boat, his back towards her, apparently doing

28

something with the tiller. His own crossbred Sandy, ears alert for adventure, sat beside him and when he saw Stone he jumped off the boat on to the path and ran up to greet him. They were old friends.

Henry turned to see what had been the object of Sandy's interest and he saw Stone before he saw Becky who, feeling suddenly ill at ease, had stopped to gaze at the scene before her.

'Hi!' Henry casually raised a hand in greeting. Then he carefully drew the tiller into the boat before getting up and stepping ashore, still clad in the outfit she had seen him in that morning. Slowly he came towards her, wiping his hands on the sides of his jeans. 'This is nice,' he said. 'Unexpected.'

'I didn't come to see you,' Becky said hastily.

'Of course not.' There was the slightest trace of sarcasm in his voice.

'Sorry, that sounds rude.' She bit her lip. 'I didn't mean to be, Henry.'

'I know you didn't.' The inflection of his voice changed as if he understood. 'I hear Max is in America.'

'Yes, on business. Our agency has an American parent. He often goes.'

'Didn't you want to go with him?'

'He's one of the heads of the agency. I only work in the art department. Very menial.'

'Of course!' Henry drew his pipe out of a side pocket and unfurled a long waterproof

29

pouch full of choice tobacco which he began to press firmly into the bowl of the pipe. 'Care for a cup of tea?' He jerked his head in the direction of his cottage.

'Why not?' Becky suddenly felt the burden of doubt and uncertainty lifted from her and smiled at him. Henry after all was a friend, an old, old family friend. Henry and she had known each other all their lives.

Whistling for the dogs, who had gone together along the path on the track of interesting smells, Henry carefully completed lighting his pipe, watched with some fascination by Becky.

This slow lighting of the pipe seemed to sum up Henry; his easy-going, unhurried way of doing things. Not like Max who was a go-getting man, a jet-setter. Henry, why Henry was a sailor and had a sailor's slow, careful, methodical ways.

Finally he had his pipe drawing to his satisfaction and then he glanced at her and saw the expression on her face.

'Why are you smiling?'

'I'm just thinking.'

'You look,' he said peering at her closely, 'as if you've been crying.'

'What nonsense!' Angrily she drew her hand across her eyes. 'It was the wind.'

'Oh!' Henry grunted and, whistling again to the dogs, who had drawn a blank on their trail, began to walk along the path to his cottage,

Becky falling into step beside him.

'Were you going sailing?'

He glanced up at the sky. 'I wasn't sure. I think I left it a bit late. There's something wrong with the rudder anyway; the pin got snagged on something and it doesn't go into the hole. Maybe I'll get Tom Mackeson to sort it out for me tomorrow.'

'I'm sure he will.' Tom was the foreman in the Versey boatyard who often went sailing with Henry. There was obviously no hurry. Henry was never in a hurry about anything. In a way she envied him. What couldn't be done today would be done tomorrow, or the day after that. Timeless was a word for Henry.

Henry ran up the steps of the cottage ahead of her and opened the door which led directly into the sitting room. From here there was a door into the kitchen and, to one side, a staircase led to the floor above where there were two bedrooms. The bathroom was downstairs off the kitchen, having been built on to it by the previous owner.

The cottage had not been the Lamb family home. That had been a house in the town which Henry had sold when his mother died, as if he had wanted to sever all connection with what had been an unhappy past, and begin again. He had been about nineteen and Becky, then still at school, remembered his excitement at his acquisition, going over it with him. She'd even made the curtains for the downstairs rooms because she was good with her hands and enjoyed designing her own clothes. At one time she'd thought of going into fashion.

Becky now looked round with a proprietorial air as if the place half belonged to her, and when Henry went into the kitchen to put the kettle on she followed him and sat at the table, the familiar deal table where she felt quite at home.

'Did you do any work today?' she asked. He wrote in the spare room upstairs which he had turned into a study, lined with shelves and placed a big desk by the window looking out to the sea.

Henry shook his head, his pipe cold now in the corner of his mouth. He put a tea bag into each of the mugs and then went back to stand by the kettle, watching it boil.

'I'm waiting,' he said.

'Waiting for what?'

'Waiting for inspiration.' He smiled and looked at her. 'Do you get days like that?'

'Frequently.'

Becky smiled companionably as one who shared the fear that always plagued the artist, of a block which would prevent them from doing their best work.

'Oh, by the way!' Henry poured the water over the tea bags in the mugs, 'that friend of yours, Ruth, was true to her word. I had a call from her agent friend who asked me to send her what I'd written.'

'Oh, that was nice of her.'

'Very nice, I thought.' Henry completed his task and then squashed the tea bags against the side of the mugs with a spoon he'd got from a drawer. 'Very nice to go to the trouble.'

'Maybe she fancies you,' Becky said slyly.

'Who?' Henry looked up sharply.

'The agent.'

'She hasn't seen me. How could she fancy me?'

Becky had the feeling she sounded ridiculous. Henry was so practical and robust, such a deflater of nonsense and nonsensical remarks. He passed her her mug and the bottle of milk.

'Help yourself,' he said.

'Thanks.' She tipped the milk into her mug and stirred. Henry sat opposite her, his mug to his lips, eyes staring at her over the rim.

'So you were in your studio today?'

'Yup!' She nodded.

'Having a week off?'

'I came down yesterday. Back tomorrow.'

'We don't see you much at weekends any more.'

'No, I miss them. Max and I usually spend them together.'

'Of course.' Henry frowned. 'I suppose I owe you an apology Becky.'

Becky looked into her mug, conscious of the mounting tension between them. Stone had finished what was left of Sandy's dinner and

33

was now helping himself to water. A heavy old-fashioned clock on the mantelpiece ticked the passing of the minutes.

'What you said about Max wasn't very nice. It's also not true. He's *not* smooth, artificial . . . he's a very kind, caring person. You simply don't know him.'

'No. I don't.'

'And Henry.' Her tone grew urgent. 'There's *never* been anything between us. Anything at all, has there?'

'No.' He nodded.

'Just affection, as friends. I am very, very fond of you Henry.'

'But you could never think of me in *that* way?'

'It never occurred to me . . . you hinted I'd rejected you. I always thought we were friends, good friends.'

'Oh Becky!' Henry got up and smashed his fist on the table. 'Are you blind?'

'Blind?' She gasped; his sudden action had startled her.

'I've fancied you for ages, years . . . yet what could I do?'

'Do?' She felt strangely breathless.

'It's quite obvious your mum and dad despise me.'

'They do *not*,' she answered hotly.

'They do.' His eyes were smouldering. 'I am not successful. They give me odd jobs.'

'They know you want to write. They

34

understand.'

'They pity me. Oh yes ... they're kind to poor orphan Henry whom they've been so good to. God forbid he should *ever* cast eyes on their only daughter.'

'Henry!' Becky rose sharply, looking around for Stone's lead. 'I don't understand you at *all*.'

'Then why did you come today?' He leaned almost menacingly across the table.

'I merely ...' she faltered.

'You *never* walk round to the sound. You always go up the path towards your house.'

'Occasionally I do,' she said defensively. 'As a matter of fact I thought I'd pick up Daddy from work. He's here today.'

She was quite shocked at her ability to lie so easily. Had she *really* been thinking of her father, or had she unconsciously been seeking out Henry? She didn't know. Truthfully, she didn't know.

'I want everything to be right between us,' she said suddenly. 'I want you to know that I do love Max and I'm going to marry him. There is no doubt about that. No question in my mind. But I value you, Henry, as a friend and I always want it to be like that. Thinking of you being miserable makes me miserable.'

'Oh *thank you*,' he said sarcastically.

'It does. It has nothing to do with my parents or what you think they do or do not think about you. They do not pity you. They *like* you. I think they've been very good to you.'

35

'Patronising.'

'They did not mean to be. They'd be terribly hurt if they knew you thought that. I think it's unfair of you, hurtful too. Just because they help it doesn't mean they patronise.'

'How do you think *I* feel then?' He walked rapidly round the table so that he stood beside her. 'The man with the wheelbarrow, sweeping up the leaves. Down come your smart friends from London. Your fiancé with the Porsche. Do you think your parents did *me* any favours inviting me to your party, or did they just want to rub my nose in it?'

'Rub your nose in *what*?' Becky was aware that her own temper was mounting.

'In my situation. In the fact that I was the frog and he was the prince who had got the princess.'

'Frogs turn into princes,' she said in an effort to defuse the situation.

'Not this time they didn't. I'm sorry they asked me. I'm sorry I went. Sorry I asked you to dance and saw the look that Max gave me when he claimed you back. Above all,' he lowered his voice, 'I'm sorry I said what I did. I really am. I gave the game away, told you the truth . . .'

'The truth?' Becky's voice was scarcely above a whisper.

'Work it out for yourself,' Henry said roughly, finishing his tea and glancing at his watch. 'I'd better go and fix that rudder before dark. The yard will be closing.'

'Right!' Conscious of the change in the atmosphere Becky gathered her things together again.

'Are you going to walk round and see your father?'

'No.'

'Right.' He took her mug and placed it in the sink with his. His manner now was different, impersonal, almost carefree. 'I'm glad we had this out,' he said.

'What did we have out? I'm not quite sure.' Becky looked puzzled.

'I think we cleared the air. We know where we are. You know how I feel.'

'Feel?' She felt more bewildered than ever.

'About your parents, my place in the house. I'm not going on any more with it Becky. No more odd jobs. I've got my pride to consider. My self-esteem. I didn't realise it before, but I do now. Tell your mother for me, will you, that I shan't be coming any more?'

'She'll miss you,' Becky said sadly as they walked together to the door, the dogs obediently at their heels.

She didn't add that so would she.

CHAPTER THREE

Leaning across the barrier in the arrival hall at Heathrow Becky was aware of the same thrilling sense of anticipation she had had as a

37

small child on Christmas Eve or the night before her birthday; the sensation that, when she opened her eyes in the morning, the world would have been magically transformed.

That intense feeling was part of the innocence of childhood and, inevitably, it grew less as one got older until at length it vanished altogether. But now, her eyes on the door leading from customs, the old feeling of excitement welled up in her chest at the thought that at any moment Max would emerge.

The doors opened and a trickle of passengers from the BA aircraft began to come through, some hesitantly, some with the same air of expectation as herself. It was fascinating watching the reactions of the travellers looking around, perhaps for loved ones or, more prosaically perhaps, the driver who was meeting them to take them to a business appointment in central London. Some seemed to have no purpose at all and no one to meet them.

And here . . . She gazed with some stupefaction at Max as he came through the door, not looking round for her as she had expected, but chatting with some animation to a tall, elegant woman, dressed in a business suit, a lock of her fashionably cut hair trailing across her left cheek. She was about thirty, impeccably made up. Max was pushing the trolley which obviously contained their baggage and she carried a handbag, a black crocodile briefcase under an arm.

Becky started towards them but Max, unseeing, passed right by her, the back of his head to her as he talked to the woman, who thus presented herself full face to Becky. Without knowing who she was, she seemed to be looking straight towards her. The stranger was a dark beauty with luminous brown eyes, high cheekbones and scarlet lips. She had the figure of a model. Perhaps she was.

Becky hesitated, not quite knowing what to do. She followed the couple from the other side of the barrier and just as they reached the exit the woman seemed to be pointing her out to Max and he turned abruptly, saw Becky and waved.

'Becky darling!' he called out, 'what a lovely surprise.'

But he didn't sweep her into his arms. As she came up to him he kissed her briefly on the lips and turned to the woman beside him.

'Lee, may I introduce to you my fiancée, Becky? I thought she was still in Hampshire with her family. Darling,' he turned to Becky, 'this is Lee Wylde, who is creative director of the New York company. She's over here for six months to teach us a thing or two.'

'To learn plenty I guess.' Lee's sanitised smile showed perfectly-formed gleaming teeth and she tossed back her head as if in an effort to dislodge the thick curl on her cheek, displaying a sculptured throat and neck.

'How do you do?' Becky held out a hand.

'Lovely of you to meet me darling.' Max kept one hand on the trolley and tucked an arm through Becky's. 'When did you come up from Hampshire?'

'Yesterday,' Becky replied.

'And how are your mother and father?'

'Fine.'

'And the painting?'

'Good.' She nodded. 'How was America?'

'Fine.' He half turned, then stopped and looked into her eyes. 'But I missed you.'

'I missed you too.'

Looking past him she saw Lee watching them with a detached smile on her face of tolerant amusement, such as one has when children are playing. Becky glanced down at her hands and saw that she wore no wedding ring.

A beautiful creative director ... unmarried—or perhaps she was divorced?

Lee consulted her watch. 'Look Max, there is no need for me to interrupt your welcome home. I can easily get a cab to the hotel.'

'Nonsense. I have my car here. We'll take you, won't we Becky?'

'Sure.' Becky nodded vigorously.

'And then we'll take you out to dinner.'

'Oh I *couldn't* ...'

'Your first night here? Don't be silly! After all, look what you did for me in New York.'

Becky's eyes glazed over but Lee maintained that perfect, almost maddening smile.

'Well, that was only in the course of business, Max.'

'So is this.' Max smiled at her and clasped Becky's hand. 'We couldn't let Lee spend her first night in London alone could we darling?'

'Of course not.' Becky shook her head.

'That's settled then. Now if you ladies would like to wait here I'll go and get the car. Give me ten minutes and I'll see you outside.' Max pointed to the doors leading on to the pavement, and without another word he was gone.

Lee suddenly seemed rather embarrassed and gave Becky a deprecating look.

'I'm *terribly* sorry. I guess this spoilt the homecoming.'

'Don't be silly. Of course not. He didn't expect me anyway.'

'No, I suppose not.' Lee's voice faltered. 'He didn't say he was expecting you to meet him.'

'It was to be a surprise. I came in on the train.'

'I feel I've really spoilt it for you.'

'Not at all. Tell me about the visit to New York. It was a success?'

'Oh very successful. Max is so admired in the States. If you ask me he's being groomed for big things.'

'Oh?'

'Maybe take over the agency entirely here, in

41

a year or two of course.' She looked mysterious.

'Really, over Ted Levine?' Levine was the UK head of the agency.

'Over Ted,' Lee said firmly. 'He doesn't go down too well in the States. He hasn't got Max's,' she paused, 'charisma. Charisma is everything in the advertising world you know Becky.'

'I know,' Becky replied with an edge to her voice. 'Max may not have mentioned it but I work for the agency too.'

'Really?' Lee looked genuinely taken aback.

'I'm a visualiser in the art department.'

'Why that's great!' Lee enthusiastically clasped her arm. 'I'm going to be your new boss. I'm the creative director in London for the next six months.'

*   *   *

'I don't think you mentioned me to her at all.'

'Of *course* I mentioned you.'

'I don't believe you.'

'Don't then.'

'Oh Max what a miserable homecoming.' Becky sank dejectedly on to the side of the bed as Max stood in front of the mirror critically examining his face as he undid his tie.

'Well *you're* making it miserable darling. In fact you've been like a wet blanket all night.'

'Thank you.'

'It's true.' He finished undoing his tie and, slinging it over the back of the chair, came and sat down beside her. 'You've behaved like a spoilt child. Sullen, silent . . .'

'Frankly I could find little to say amid the torrent of words we had from Lee.'

'I think she felt awkward. People talk too much when they're embarrassed.'

'Look Max,' Becky turned and faced him, 'why didn't you tell me she was coming?'

'I didn't know until the last minute. I thought she was coming on a later plane. Besides, I didn't know you'd be there. I thought you were at home all week. If it had been a man I wouldn't have had this stupid, childish reaction from you.'

'I do resent that.' Becky got to her feet and walked over to the window, gazing out on to the dark rain-soaked Hampstead street beneath Max's apartment. Despite the central heating, she felt cold. Maybe she *had* behaved like a child. Maybe she lacked the womanly wiles of someone as sophisticated as Lee. 'Okay maybe I'm jealous! I'm sorry.' She turned to Max, who had slumped on the bed gazing at the floor.

'You wear your heart on your sleeve darling.' He looked critically up at her.

'Is that so wrong?'

'It's not good for business. My business, *our* business,' he corrected himself. 'In fact you might have faxed me that you were coming and this wouldn't have happened.'

'You mean you'd have caught a different plane?'

'No, I don't mean that. I would have warned you that I was bringing the boss's daughter over and asked you to give her a better welcome than the one you did.'

'The boss's daughter! You don't mean she's the daughter of Daryl Peake? But Wylde . . .'

'Wylde is her married name. She's divorced, of course, but she kept the name so that people would not associate her with her father. If I'd known you would be there I'd have prepared you. Darling I'm sorry.' He got up and came and stood behind her, his hands closing on her shoulders, his mouth nuzzling her cheek. 'Look it's been a bad start. We're both tired. Let's go to bed and forget all about it.'

*   *   *

She tried but she couldn't. No use pretending to enjoy lovemaking that night with Max. He felt her lack of responsiveness and in the end he gave up himself and lay beside her, tense and frustrated.

'I can't be something I'm not,' Becky said. 'I can't pretend.'

'That's all too obvious.'

She thought of Lee lying, no doubt, in the bed in her elegant suite in the Churchill Hotel with that superior little smile on her face. She

44

was the sort of woman that other women would try and like but never could. A man's woman.

A man's woman, and her boss.

* * *

Becky got to the office early but even then someone had been there before her. On her desk by her drawing board was a vase in which there was an enormous bunch of flowers. Sarah, who sat at the next desk to her, smiled and turned round twice in her chair.

'But *who*?' Becky gazed at the flowers and then saw the card propped in front of it.

'Someone likes you,' Sarah said as Becky took up the card and slit open the envelope.

'Thank you so much for your lovely welcome. I'm going to enjoy working with you. Lee.'

'Lee!' Becky threw the card down on the desk and gazed at the flowers, tempted to hurl them into the wastepaper basket.

'She's charming!' Sarah glanced at her slyly. 'Or don't you think so?'

'Oh *I* think so,' Becky said casually. 'She came over with Max.'

'She told me. She brought the flowers in herself and said how kind you'd been.'

45

'*Kind*!' Becky took up a pencil and threw it down again. 'I behaved like a child. I feel bad about it. Max despises me.'

'I'm sure he doesn't. I understand your feelings because she's very glamorous.'

'He came over on the plane with her. I wasn't prepared. He obviously didn't expect to see me and then when he did he looked disconcerted. He quickly made up for it but, Sarah, I don't believe he *ever* mentioned me to Lee as his fiancée.'

'Oh I'm sure he did,' Sarah said loyally.

'She seemed completely unprepared for me. She didn't know I worked here and I'm sure she didn't know Max was even engaged.'

'Maybe it was strictly a business trip and he didn't like to mention it. Men are funny creatures.' Sarah sniffed derisively with the air of one who knew. She had been married for five years and had just left her husband. 'Look,' she turned to Becky, 'why don't you go and thank her and act all sophisticated?'

'Because I can't. I'm not like her.' Becky looked down at the jeans and T-shirt she wore for work. They were *de rigueur* in the art department. 'Do you know I'm thinking of chucking in this job altogether?'

'And do what?'

'Paint. I'd have to leave it anyway when we're married.' She paused. '*If* we marry.'

'Of course you're going to marry! Max loves you. He *adores* you. Why yesterday you could hardly work for excitement.'

'That was yesterday.' Becky crossed her arms and looked out of the window, past the tall buildings that stood between the City tower where they worked and the river. The dome of St Paul's Cathedral looked like a small speck in the distance. Suddenly she thought of home and the bay, of Stone rushing headlong across the beach, and a lump came into her throat. 'I guess I have been a child,' she said slowly, 'not quite grown up enough for Max.'

*   *   *

Quietly she closed the door and as she did she was aware of the fragrance that emanated from the woman who had crossed the floor to meet her, arms warmly extended.

'I just wanted to thank you for the flowers,' Becky said. 'It was a very sweet thought. You really shouldn't.'

'Oh but I should,' Lee protested, taking her arm and guiding her to one of the soft, expensive chairs in front of her desk. The managing director Ted Levine had given her his office and moved to a smaller one across the corridor. Now it was filled with the same kinds of flowers that stood on Becky's desk, and she guessed that Lee had gone round collecting a few choice blooms and had made up a bouquet for her.

Still, it was the thought that counted, wasn't

it?

'I can't tell you how much I appreciated last night Becky.' She leaned towards her, hands joined across her desk. 'I realised how you must have felt having been separated for two whole weeks from Max. It was really kind of you to give up your evening for me. I guess I would have felt a little lonesome. And I loved the restaurant you took me to.'

'We loved having you,' Becky said woodenly.

'And your *work*!' Lee turned enthusiastically to the table by her desk and produced a sample of the artwork that Becky had recently finished for a campaign to promote a new brand of wholesome packet soups. 'It's superb. You're really an artist. Max says you paint very well.'

'Mostly views of the bay.' Becky scratched her head. 'A few still lifes, this and that.'

'He said you have a wonderful home by the sea.'

'Oh, he told you all that?' Becky looked interested. Perhaps she had misjudged Max after all.

'This morning.' Lee gazed down at her desk. 'I wanted to thank him for last night too. He's the perfect host and I think he's *just* the person to take over from Ted when he retires.'

'Retires?' Becky looked surprised. 'Ted is only—'

'Takes *early* retirement,' Lee said quickly. 'I believe his health's not too good.'

'I didn't realise of course that Daryl Peake is

48

your father.'

'No. It's best not noised abroad. Max told you, of course, but do you think you could keep it a secret?'

'I could try.' Becky seemed unconvinced. 'But things like that get round. For instance, you moving into Ted's office is rather significant, even if you are the creative director.'

'He insisted.' Lee laughed and, rising, crossed to the window. 'Really everyone has been so *kind* and,' she turned to Becky, 'I'm sure you and I will be great friends.' She sat down next to her and put a hand familiarly on her arm. 'Tell me, when's the wedding?'

*   *   *

'Lee really is trying hard,' Max said. 'Everyone likes her. Do you like her darling?'

'A little better.' Becky, her eyes on the TV at the foot of the bed, acquiesced. It was Sunday, their Sunday, with the papers piled up on the bed and the remnants of a good brunch on the table in the kitchen. Becky finished the peach she was eating and carefully put the stone on the plate by her side before wiping her hands. 'She's very capable.'

'She likes your work.'

Becky nodded.

'And you.' Max flicked off the TV with the remote control and rolled over the bed towards

49

her. 'She specially likes *you*. She thinks you've got a lot of talent.' His hands slid gently between her legs. 'I think you have too.'

'Oh *Max*!'

She lay back as his arms encircled her, his mouth pressed down on hers, aware of her desire, her longing for him.

Afterwards her head rested on his chest and his fingers played idly with her hair. They were both replete, deeply satisfied.

'I think that was the best lovemaking we've ever had,' he murmured.

'Me too.' She felt content, happy, all her fears had evaporated.

'I love you Becky.'

'And I love you.'

'Let's get married soon.'

'Soon?' She opened her eyes and looked at him. 'Sooner than next May?'

'Why not? I think Lee would rather like to be present.'

'Oh!' Suddenly she felt rage in her heart, a lump in her throat. The name of Lee was never very far away. 'Are you sure?'

'I think she'd like it. She is very important to me you know, to my career. A big wedding at Steethey would go down very well.'

'Really?' The cold seemed to travel from her feet to the tip of her head.

'Well we were going to have a big wedding anyway weren't we darling?' He propped himself up on his elbow. 'You know, a fuss for the family. Your father's only daughter, that kind of thing.'

'I suppose so.'

'You don't sound at all keen. Don't you *want* to marry me?'

'Of course I want to marry you, silly.' She reached for his hand but the cold sensation still didn't go away. 'I just don't want to do it for *Lee*.'

'But you said you liked her better.'

'I do, but I don't want to get married for her. For heaven's sake Max.' She jumped up on the bed and angrily faced him. 'I think that woman obsesses you.'

'She does not. I think she obsesses *you*.'

'You're always in her office. Everyone is talking about it.'

'We're always having meetings, Becky. You know that I'm being groomed to replace Ted. And I'll tell you another thing, *she* is being groomed to succeed her father. There. What do you think of that? The old man is retiring and his daughter will take his place.'

'No wonder you're sucking up to her.'

'I am *not* sucking up to her! I'm just doing what any sensible, ambitious man would, and if you had any sense, any feeling for my career, you'd help me. Darling—' his hand reached for hers, 'don't let's row. You can't possibly doubt my love for you, my commitment to you. But I am ambitious for us both Becky. Do you realise what being head of the agency in England would do for my career? Can you imagine how wealthy we'll be? Why the world is my oyster, and with you beside me—' He paused as he pressed her hand to his lips. 'Darling do you think we could invite Lee down to Steethey for the weekend? I think she'd get on so well with your father. It would impress her, you know . . . his success, his title. The Americans love that sort of thing.'

CHAPTER FOUR

Becky sat at the stern of Henry's sailing dinghy, one hand on the tiller, the sheet of the mainsail between fingers and thumb of the other. In the bows Henry sat on the side of the boat leaning as far back as he could to steady her in a choppy sea. He cast his eyes anxiously towards the sky.

'Maybe we should turn back. The sea's whipping up to force four. I have a responsibility to Max to deliver you safely back.'

'Not yet!' Becky deliberately ignored his last remark. 'It's just so lovely to be here, away from her.'

'Then *why* did you ask her down?'

'Max wanted it. He wants to impress her with his in-laws-to-be. He thought she would get on with Daddy.'

'And does she?'

'Oh yes! Lee gets on with everyone. She's the perfect mixer. Even Stone likes her.'

'But you don't!' Henry leaned towards her and smiled. 'Do I detect jealousy?'

'Perhaps. I'm trying very hard; but why do some women make others feel inadequate? Do you know what I mean?'

'It would be interesting to meet her. Well, quite.' Henry seemed unconvinced of his own curiosity. Or maybe it was from a desire not to upset Becky.

'Well you will tonight. Mummy wants you to come to dinner.'

'Oh, *no* thank you.' Henry vigorously shook his head.

'Go on, please.'

'Definitely not.'

'I really need you Henry. I do.'

For answer Henry thoughtfully scanned the skies again and looked back at the receding coastline.

'Let's go about,' he said, 'and make for home.'

Becky drew the tiller towards her, changed hands with the mainsail sheet and, ducking to avoid the boom as it swung over, transferred to the other side of the boat while at the bow Henry did the same so that once again he was opposite her. Ahead of them now was the coastline and the familiar sight of Steethey House perched on the clifftop. It was very far away but Becky thought she could discern figures on the lawn and imagined that her parents were showing Lee the garden.

'Well?' she said, looking at Henry. 'You didn't answer my question.'

'I'm not coming to dinner,' he said firmly. 'You know how I feel.'

'You still have this "thing" about being patronised.'

'I had. I haven't now.'

'What are you getting up to now that you're no longer doing the garden?'

'This and that.'

'Very helpful,' Becky said sarcastically. 'There's no need to take it out on me as well as my family, Henry. I do want us still to be friends.'

Henry ignored her remark and said, 'I *may* go into the boat business. It's something I know a lot about. Oh not building,' he smiled at the expression on her face, 'but chartering. I thought I might get a proper yacht, you know, one that sleeps four or six, and charter it in the summer. By that time I should know if I'm going to succeed with my writing or not and even if I do it will give me a second string. As a matter of fact . . .' he groped in his pocket for his pipe and then seemed to think better of it because of the wind, 'I don't know why I didn't think of it before.'

They fell silent again, a companionable silence broken only by the sound of gulls and the boat slicing through the water.

The wind, coming from the south, filled their sails with air, and on a close reach Becky kept the dinghy on a steady course until it was time to lower the mainsail and go into the harbour on the jib.

Henry watched her with approval as she steered the boat expertly into its bay, and as he secured the painter to a buoy in the harbour Becky undid the rudder and examined it.

'Seems fine now.'

'Yes, they did a bit of welding up at your yard. You know Becky you're a good yachtswoman. I could use you as crew on my yacht.'

'Thanks,' she said with a smile. 'If ever it comes to it I'll remember that.'

They stowed away the sails, unfastened the boom and placed it in the bottom of the boat, then, with a final look round, Henry vaulted on to the jetty and held out his hand to assist Becky. As she grabbed his hand she missed her footing, falling heavily against him; but instead of pulling her up he drew her head towards his chest and planted a kiss firmly on her brow.

'Henry!' Becky struggled to regain her footing but Henry held fast on to her and, tilting her chin, brought her mouth up to his. '*Henry!*' she cried again, putting a hand firmly on his face and pushing him away. To her consternation she found she was trembling. 'You mustn't do that!'

'Why not?'

'Because I'm engaged. The rules of engagement prevent me making love to another man. Don't you understand that?'

He still didn't release her wrist, but with a sardonic disbelieving expression gazed into her eyes.

'Are you *really* in love with Max Lavery?'

'Yes, I am.'

'No doubts at all?'

'Absolutely none.'

'I don't believe you. You're like a cat on hot bricks. He doesn't give you any security does he?'

'Love isn't about security,' she said defensively, yet not afraid to meet his eyes.

'I think it is. It's about loving and being loved. You seem to doubt Max's love.'

'Well I don't.'

'Why, then, are you so worried about Lee?'

'It's natural to be jealous of another woman, especially if she's sophisticated, beautiful *and* the boss's daughter.' Becky tried to keep her tone bantering.

'I don't think it is.' Finally he let go her hand and, reaching into the boat for his satchel, swung it over his shoulder. Then he produced his pipe from his pocket and slowly began to fill it. 'You're going to meet many beautiful and sophisticated women in your life once you're married to Max, with the kind of work you do. You can't go on being jealous of them *all*. If so you'll be a nervous wreck. Besides—' he pressed the tobacco firmly into the bowl of the pipe with his strong sailor's fingers, 'it's not like you. You've lost your serenity Becky.'

'Serenity!' she scoffed. 'No one ever called me "serene" before.'

'Yes!' He slowly lit his pipe and once he had it glowing to his satisfaction began to walk along the jetty with his long loping strides. 'You *had* a serenity, the sort that comes from knowing you were first class at what you did. You were an artist, a draughtswoman, good at your job. You were at ease with yourself, with the landscape around you, and it showed. Since you got engaged to Max all that has gone.'

He looked at her and she thought she saw a certain satisfaction in his eyes.

'I think *you're* the one who's jealous,' she said slowly.

'Then maybe we're both jealous.' He stopped, removing his pipe from his mouth and looking down at her. 'I'm jealous of Max, and you're jealous of Lee. There's no justice in the world is there?'

*　　　*　　　*

In a perfect world there *would* be no jealousy, Becky thought, as later that night they sat round the table for dinner. She had Max on one side, her father on the other. Lee sat between him and her mother. They were a man short which obviously distressed Lady Versey.

57

Lee wore a short black evening dress that set off the stunning marble white of her shoulders, her rounded bosom, her long, elegant throat. At another time, another place, Becky would have liked to have painted her. No one could deny that she was striking.

Sir John was captivated by her. He'd taken her round his boatyard that afternoon, showed her the garden, and tomorrow they were going to do a tour of the countryside.

'I do hate being a man short,' Margaret Versey said as they spread their napkins on their laps. Jessie, who looked after them during the day, had come in to serve the meal she and Lady Versey had cooked. She stood now with a white apron over her neat navy dress, a serving knife and fork in her hands.

'Will you serve the terrine my lady?'

'I think we'll help ourselves Jessie.' Margaret looked up at her with a smile. 'Sir John will pour the wine.'

'A Puligny-Montrachet,' Sir John said with a knowing glance at Lee. '1983. I think you'll like it.' Then, after pouring a small quantity into his glass and tasting it, he filled hers before going round the table.

'Oh *I* don't mind at all being a man short,' Lee said, looking round. 'In the States we regard that sort of thing as old-fashioned, balancing the sexes I mean. Don't you agree Max?'

'I have no particular views on the matter.'

58

Max looked at his future mother-in-law. 'It depends on who the man is.'

'We hoped Henry would come. He always fills in.'

'Henry?' Lee looked from Sir John to Lady Versey.

'Henry Lamb,' Sir John explained. 'An old family friend. Lives in a cottage on the beach. Eccentric chap.'

'Oh the man who did the *gardening!*' Max looked as though he had suddenly been enlightened. 'The gardener. Now I know who you mean.'

'Well, he helped out in the garden.' Margaret, who was something of a snob, looked embarrassed. 'He's a writer really, but he suddenly stopped gardening, without explanation, a few weeks ago. I think it was his pride.'

'Pride!' Sir John fumed. 'He left me in the lurch.'

'John we can soon get someone else. Writers *are* prickly,' Margaret explained to Lee. 'I expect you know a few.'

'I—' Lee began, but Max intervened sharply.

'A "writer", as I understand, who has never had anything published?' Beside him Becky stiffened.

'Why must you always be horrible about Henry?' she asked.

'Darling.' he expostulated, 'I am not horrible about Henry.'

'You're always demeaning him,' she insisted.

'On the contrary I hardly know him. I think you're rather sensitive about Henry.'

'Becky and Henry have known each other since they were children,' Margaret hurriedly explained, glancing apologetically at their guest. Then, with a loud sigh, 'But we do miss him. He was so good doing things about the house. He's so practical, whereas John and Miles, for all their skills at boats, are not.'

'Miles is your son?' Lee seemed anxious to change the subject.

Margaret nodded. 'Miles is in the business with John. Alas he was detained tonight in Portsmouth and couldn't join us.'

'Well one day maybe I'll meet Miles . . . and Henry.' Lee looked slyly at Max. 'I must say he sounds intriguing. *Is* he intriguing, Becky?'

'Not a bit,' Becky said robustly. 'He's just Henry.'

'But didn't you go sailing with him this afternoon? I think we saw you in the bay, didn't we Sir John?'

'We did indeed.' John looked at his daughter with pride. 'Becky's a fine sailor. Pity you don't like sailing, Max. I could have given you a boat for a wedding present.'

'Thanks, but no thanks.' Max gave a deprecating laugh. 'I like my feet on dry land.'

'What about the air?' Becky said.

'What *about* the air, darling?' Max gave an exaggerated sigh.

'You like flying and that's not dry land . . .'

'It's—'

'Oh dear you two *are* argumentative this evening,' Margaret tutted, giving a distracted laugh.

'Lovers' tiffs,' Sir John said jovially.

'Talking about weddings . . .' Max reached for Becky's hand, 'we wondered about bringing forward the date. Would you mind, Lady Versey?'

'Bring forward the date!' Margaret Versey looked flustered. 'Not the spring?'

'We thought a winter wedding, and a honeymoon in Klosters.'

'Well *I've* nothing against a winter wedding.' Margaret still sounded dubious. 'Have you John?'

'The sooner the better,' John said, 'if that's what the happy couple want.'

'What fun! I shall be here for it,' Lee exclaimed. 'That would be lovely. I can take a video of it and show it to Daddy when I get home.' Then, turning pointedly to her host, 'You know, Sir John, we think a *great* deal of Max.'

'John, *please.*'

'You know, John, we think a *great* deal of Max. Within two years he will be head of the agency in England.'

'That's splendid news,' Margaret gazed at her future son-in-law with pride, 'and so exciting for Becky. Darling, if the wedding is to be brought forward oughtn't we to be thinking of plans now? This very moment?'

Becky felt a constriction in her throat as she answered. 'I suppose so.'

'And your work. Won't you be giving it up?'

'Oh, we should hate to lose her.' Lee clasped her hands together in alarm. 'Becky is so gifted. But I do understand. Maybe she can work on a freelance basis?'

'You sound as though I've left already,' Becky demurred. 'I'd like to finish the visuals I'm doing at the moment, anyway.'

'Of course, take all the time that you want,' Lee said graciously, as if that settled the matter. '*Delicious* terrine, Lady Versey.'

'Margaret.'

'Delicious terrine, Margaret.'

*　　　*　　　*

Becky stood for a long time by the window looking out on to the sea shimmering in the moonlight. It cast a long, fluorescent beam in which there was some dark object, maybe a fishing boat. She wondered if Henry would take the dinghy out at night? But no, he never would. Always Henry, somewhere there in her thoughts. The room was in darkness and she knew that Max was lying there, waiting impatiently for her to come to bed. The view from her bedroom window was slightly different from the studio, looking south and west with an aspect of the cliffs as well as the sea.

'Come to bed darling. I'm lonely.'

She loved this place, this house, this view. When they were married it could never be the same again. They would live in Max's flat and undoubtedly there would be a country house, maybe in the Thames valley which he liked. She thought that was mainly because of the social life as so many people like him lived there: people in advertising, the media, people whose lifestyles fitted in with his. And hers?

If the wedding *were* brought forward she would be his wife in three short months.

She took off her dressing-gown and throwing it over a chair climbed into bed beside him.

'I like you nude,' Max said, lifting up her nightie. 'Take it off.'

Obediently she raised it above her head and tossed it on the floor beside her. With one hand he caressed her breasts, the other slid insinuatingly between her legs.

Oh Max, if only I could love you like I used to, she thought.

'Becky?'

'Mmm?'

'Still in a mood?'

'I'm not in a mood.'

'I think you are in a mood, darling. I think there's something wrong.' He removed one hand, but left the other on her breast. He propped himself on an elbow and she was

63

aware of his strong, stern profile in the moonlight. In the past she would have reached out, been hungry for his kisses. But not now, not tonight.

'Are you in love with Henry?'

'Of course I'm not in love with Henry!'

'What is it then?'

There was no answer.

'Is it Lee?'

'Are you in love with Lee?' She turned to him.

'Of course I'm not! What an absurd question.'

'Well that's how I feel when you ask me about Henry. He's like a piece of furniture. You've only just met Lee.'

'I have not only just met Lee.'

'Oh!' She hadn't thought of that. 'You see her every time you go to the States?'

'Of course. She's been the creative director for five years.'

'I see. You knew her husband then?'

'Yes, a very decent sort of bloke called Paul.'

'When did they split up?'

'About a year ago.'

'So then she became "available"?'

'Not to me!'

His mouth bore down upon hers. She tried to push him away but he grew more demanding, thrusting his hand so fiercely inside her that he hurt her. She tried to grab it but it was like a bar of steel.

'I can't—' she tried to say.

'You *can* and you *will*.' His other hand pressed firmly over her mouth and then, expertly positioning himself between her open thighs, he stretched his body the length of hers. 'You can and you will! I've had enough of this playacting. You've been like a silly schoolgirl since Lee arrived, jealous and stupid. How do you think it makes *me* feel?'

Terrified, she couldn't have replied even if she wanted to. She had a feeling of strangulation, her senses drowning.

'It makes me feel stupid that's what!' He lurched violently into her. 'Goodness knows what Lee makes of you. I want a wife I can be proud of, show off to people, not a schoolgirl asking awkward questions, mooning about over another man.'

He thrust harder and harder, hurting her as he never had before, careless of her feelings or her pleasure.

And in the room next door she imagined Lee reading in the subdued lamplight with the quiet self-satisfied smile on her face, oblivious to the turmoil going on but a few feet away.

*   *   *

Becky hadn't thought she would sleep a wink but somehow she did. Sore and bruised, wounded in body and soul, she had expected to lie awake beside the man she felt had raped

65

her, until, at dawn, she would creep out and go down to the sea and, even in those cold autumnal waters, wash herself of the shame and humiliation he'd inflicted on her.

However, somehow, sleep she did and when she woke up it was long past dawn and she could see outside the blue sky and sunshine. She turned her head and saw Max gazing at her, his face solemn, his eyes dark with foreboding. He put out his hand and she cried softly, 'Don't touch me, please!'

'I'm sorry.' He turned on his back and gazed at the ceiling. To her amazement she saw tears trickle out of the corner of his eyes. 'I was like a beast. I am truly, truly sorry.'

She didn't know what to say but, as the tears continued to flow, she was suddenly overwhelmed not with rage but with pity. What would Lee say if she could see him now! But she knew that Lee would never see him like this, because Max would never take Lee by violence. He would never attempt it and, more importantly, she would never permit it.

Why then had she, Becky, permitted it? Because she didn't want to make a fuss, disturb the house, upset her mother and father, to say nothing of their important guest? Was *that* why, when he had finished, she hadn't rushed out of bed, flung open the door and found another bed for the night? Miles's, for instance, since he was in Portsmouth overnight?

Instead Max had turned his back to her and

gone promptly to sleep and she had lain there, frightened and bruised, a person alone in the world, conscious of her isolation instead of feeling surrounded by family and friends who loved her.

She had not wanted to betray Max and now, as she saw how aware he was of the consequences of his behaviour, she felt sorry for him.

Maybe this was what love was? One had to forgive, to take the bad as well as the good. It was what she would have to promise in her marriage vows: for better or worse.

'Max!' She turned on her side and leaned over him, dabbing at his tears with a corner of the sheet.

'Oh darling Becky.' He reached out gratefully for her hand. 'Do say you forgive me. I thought when I woke this morning you wouldn't be here, but you are. I was so ashamed that in a way I was hoping you wouldn't be.'

'What did you think I would do?'

'I didn't know. Show me up to your mother and father, to Lee . . . I was a beast. I would have deserved it. All I can say is that I lost control, completely.'

'I've been a silly fool,' Becky said slowly, putting a hand on his arm. 'I *have* behaved like a jealous little schoolgirl and I made you mad.'

'It doesn't explain, or excuse my behaviour.'

She felt then that she loved him with an

overwhelming love, a love that forgave all manner of things. Relations between people were never simple; there were no easy answers. He had hurt and abused her but she . . . no she didn't *deserve* it. Nothing really excused a man taking a woman by force, unless one tried to understand the meaning of desire, the harsh, elemental forces of nature.

'It will *never* happen again.' He pressed her hand to his mouth. 'Oh Becky, say you forgive me?'

'I forgive you,' she said and then, in a voice only slightly less certain, 'I love you, Max.'

CHAPTER FIVE

Becky sat at the back of the room with her colleagues from the art department. Dressed informally, like Becky, they tended to lounge in their seats, unlike the account executives and marketing personnel who wore business suits, and sat upright, with clipboards or notepads on their knees.

Nothing seemed to Becky to differentiate this approach to their work so much as the way they dressed. The art department was relaxed, creative, iconoclastic. The executives were disciplined, well organised, future pillars of the Establishment.

Lee was exquisitely turned out, as usual, in a round-necked designer suit and two strings of pearls. Next to her, Max, cheeks freshly shaved, thick hair curling slightly behind his ears, wore a grey pinstripe suit, a white shirt with a button-down collar that he'd bought in America, and a grey tie with a fine red stripe in it.

Max was near the top of the tree, already a success; deputy director of the agency, being groomed by the woman beside him, for the top. They looked a very good pair, Becky thought, and idly she started to sketch them on her clipboard, and the likenesses were so good that Sarah, next to her, leaned over and giggled. If anything it was a caricature, with a very large Lee and a diminutive Max looking up at her with an expression of exaggerated respect.

'Perfect!' Sarah whispered, and then after a pause, 'but I thought you *loved* him?'

Becky didn't answer but, realising that cruel as it was, it could give a misleading impression, she hurriedly scribbled over the drawing and, ignoring Sarah, raised her head attentively to hear what the creative director was saying.

As it happened it was about her.

'Becky's artwork for the soup campaign is really excellent,' she said, holding up the finished drawings. 'I like the caption too— "There's so much you can do with soup". Who was responsible for that Max?'

Max gave a deprecating cough, hand in front of his mouth.

'I was actually, Lee.'

'Ah, a good team working together. I see.'

She beamed with approval and then consulted her notes. 'But this does lead me to make a rather sad announcement.' She replaced the artwork on her desk and looked at the assembled group. 'Becky will soon be leaving. Her marriage to Max is being brought forward. Naturally there's a lot to do. Of course we're very happy for them both, but sad to lose Becky. However, I am pleased to tell you that she will be working for us on a freelance basis, so we will not be losing her altogether.' One or two faces were turned to her and the head of the art department winked.

'That is all I have to say I think this morning, ladies and gentlemen,' Lee concluded. 'Except to say that Ted Levine is on indefinite sick leave, and as Max is going to Italy for a few weeks to explore new opportunities there, I shall be acting head of the agency for a short while. Please any of you feel free to come and see me any time you wish.'

The meeting broke up and Sarah and Becky wandered back to the art department and sat down at their desks.

'There's *so* much you can do with soup.' Becky made a face and, screwing the spoiled drawing into a ball, pitched it into the wastepaper basket. 'What a swan song.'

'Swan song?' Sarah looked curiously at her.

'My last full-time campaign over a packet of measly soup.

'Very nourishing,' Sarah commented,

looking at the drawing of an animated family group peering into a large bowl full of steaming liquid. It was extremely lifelike. Becky had a very unusual, quirky style rather like a comic strip with clean-cut lines and the use of bright, primary colours. The animated expressions on the faces of the participants were all exaggerated and it could be that she was almost, but not quite, taking the mickey out of the situation. However, her clients had accepted it and it would appear it was now going to the film department to be animated.

'So Max is going to Italy?'

'Yes.' Becky pulled open the drawer of her desk.

'But not with you?'

'No.'

'I shall miss you terribly,' Sarah sighed.

'And I shall miss you.'

'What made you bring the date forward?'

'Max was keen.'

'And you?' Sarah looked searchingly at her. 'Are you keen?'

'Of course.'

'That drawing was a bit ... unflattering.' Sarah indicated the wastepaper basket.

'That's why I screwed it up and threw it away.'

'It isn't that you don't like Lee?'

'Let's say I like her better than I did. I think underneath that brittle veneer she is quite fragile. Max thinks so anyway.'

71

'Of course it wasn't strictly necessary for you to leave.' Sarah began to doodle on a piece of blank paper in front of her. 'In fact, don't you think it's rather chauvinistic that you are expected to quit your job and not Max?'

'I'm not "expected" to,' Becky said defensively. 'I actually rather wanted to. I'm quite happy to leave. I'd like to give more time to my painting anyway. In many ways advertising is not only unfulfilling, it's idiotic.'

'Hush, heresy!' Sarah looked nervously towards the door.

'Anyway, Lee seemed to think it was the right thing to do.'

'You don't imagine she . . .' Sarah scribbled frantically on the paper in front of her.

'Yes?'

'Well, she wants to get rid of you?' Sarah opened her eyes very wide.

'She just told me I was very good.'

'Maybe out of the way, because of Max?'

'That's a bitchy remark,' Becky said. 'I thought you were my friend?'

'It's *because* I'm your friend that I want to alert you to something you might not be aware of. People say—' Sarah nervously crossed and uncrossed her legs, 'people *say* they spend an awful lot of time together.'

'I know that. They have to. Look, Sarah, I know what's on your mind and I know things haven't been all that easy the last few weeks, but now I feel as confident of Max as I ever did.

We had a sort of crisis recently that brought things to the boil. I can't really talk about it, but having got over it, I feel our love is stronger than ever.'

*   *   *

Before she left that evening, Becky retrieved the defaced cartoon from the wastepaper basket, just in case Sarah should want to retrieve it and do her damage with it.

*   *   *

It was early morning, a good time to make love. As they clung together she thought that his gentle, rhythmic movements were like the breaking of the waves, the gentle wash upon the shore. In her mind's eye she saw the Steethey coastline stretched out before her, the gulls dipping low, the prow of the boat pointed seawards. Henry aloof, alone, casting his seasoned sailor's eyes to the scudding clouds overhead.

Henry. Why should she even *think* of Henry when, eventually, her head lay on Max's breast and he made soothing noises in her ear, whispering that he loved her?

'But I love you too,' she whispered back and then she closed her eyes and felt like crying.

'Darling?' Detecting the change in mood he lifted her chin with his finger, saw the suspicion of tears moist on her cheek.

'I'm going to miss you Max.'

'I shan't be gone long.'

'By the time you come back I'll have left the agency.'

'And we'll be that much nearer to getting married. Think of that!'

'Will Lee be joining you in Italy?'

'I don't know. She might.' Gently he released her and sat up. 'She might come to Milan because there's some sort of advertising fair. Look darling—' Max took his watch from the bedside table and examined it closely as if conscious of the passing of time, 'it would be awfully nice of you to invite Lee to Steethey while I'm away and get to know her better. It would be good for my career also. Make sure,' he glanced at her, 'that she doesn't forget *you*.'

'Forget me?' Becky looked surprised.

'I mean as an artist. You're good but we have a lot of talented people in that department. I want you to make a friend of her.'

'I don't think I could ever do that,' Becky said bleakly. Even after they'd just made love he was already thinking of Lee . . . but then she had been thinking of Henry or, rather, he had come unbidden to her mind.

'You mustn't be *negative* about Lee,' Max said rather sharply, easing himself out of bed and into his dressing-gown. 'She likes you a lot. Thinks you're talented. I tell you it's very important to keep in with her. It's a hard world out there. For you and, of course, for me. As

74

her old man is the boss it's pretty vital to my career. It's pretty important to us both.'

*　　*　　*

The car drew up outside the gate of terminal 4 and the two people in the front seats sat silently for a moment.

'I shall miss you,' the woman said turning to the man at the wheel.

'It's not for long,' he replied, feeling edgy, uncomfortable.

'Say, why don't I come and see you off, stretch my legs?' She gave a bright, artificial smile as if this was something she'd just thought of, rather than been actively planning the journey's length.

Max looked at his watch.

'We could have a drink,' she added.

'Fine,' he agreed, 'I'd like that.'

He started the engine, put the car into gear and drove round to the short-stay car park. It was a bit stupid but, after all, she was the boss. He didn't have much time, but even if he missed the plane there was sure to be another quite soon. London to Rome; planes were taking off all the time.

Lee had insisted on taking Max to the airport saying, casually, what fun it would be to try out her newly acquired Mercedes sports car.

He had intended driving himself so as to facilitate his return. But Lee had different ideas and Max had quickly discovered that it was not a very good move to cross her. She was a formidable woman with pronounced views of her own, on everything, work or play.

Even if she had not been Daryl Peake's daughter, Max had decided, she would have been successful in whatever she set out to do. In his position it was difficult to know quite how to handle her. He suspected she found him attractive, as he did her. She was sexy and it would not have taken much to push him into bed with her; but he knew that the situation was dangerous. Fail and he could lose her, his job and Becky.

And with Becky he was in love, he was sure of that.

Max Lavery was a self-made man, aware of his own limitations. His father had worked in a bank, never made it to managerial status, a teller behind the counter all his life. Max had not gone to public school. Afraid of taking after his father he had not had a good scholastic career and had left after taking two O levels.

But a lot of self-made, successful businessmen had had starts like his. By twenty he was earning far more than he would ever have earned if he had been a studious boy and gone to university. By twenty he would still have been at university, and all the entrepreneurial skills, the street-wise tricks of the advertising trade, primarily on the marketing side, that he had acquired between the ages of sixteen and twenty, would have remained unlearnt. He was sure of that. If, at twenty-one, he had been a graduate he would probably have gone into a safe job, joined a large corporation with global connections and eventually retired in some middle-managerial position.

They got out of the car and Max went round to get his bags from the boot.

'She's lovely isn't she?' Lee rested her hand on the bonnet of the car, stroking it fondly as if it were a gorgeous, vibrant animal.

'Lovely,' Max agreed.

'Do you like her better than the Porsche?'

Max shrugged and passed Lee the keys. 'To me a car is a means of getting from A to B.'

'Go on I don't believe you.' She gave him a playful tap.

'No seriously, I can't be in love with a car.'

Lee tucked an arm through Max's as they made for the exit into the main terminal. 'Not like you're in love with Becky?'

'Oh no, of course. Not like that.'

Max felt even more uncomfortable and the hand resting inside his arm made him feel uneasy too.

'I think Becky's just divine.'

'She is.' Max nodded and gently drew away from her in order to extract his ticket from his breast pocket. Reluctantly, it seemed, Lee let her arm fall.

'I'm just thrilled that she's invited me down

77

for the weekend while you're away. It means, I think, that she must really like me.'

Max was rather startled by Lee's naïveté. By the fact that Becky's approval seemed to matter so much to her. Maybe she wasn't as sophisticated as she seemed.

'Oh she does like you.'

'And I like her; I know you're going to be so happy together.'

Max didn't comment, just watched his luggage go, received his tickets and boarding pass back from the clerk, smiled at her—she was very pretty too—and looked at Lee.

'Just time for that quick drink,' he said, and then at that moment the announcement of his flight came over the tannoy. 'Perhaps not,' he grimaced. 'You'll be okay driving the car back?'

'Of course I'll be okay!' Lee exclaimed. 'I just wanted you to have the feel of her between your hands.'

It was a suggestive remark uttered, Max thought, with a suggestive nuance in her voice, but when he looked at her Lee's expression was entirely innocent and non-committal.

'Come, I'll see you to passport control,' she said, taking his arm again and then, when they reached the barrier, she leant towards him and pecked him swiftly on the cheek. 'You be careful with those Italian signorinas,' she said. 'Be sure you keep yourself pure for Becky.'

'Don't worry I will.' Now that the moment for departure had arrived Max felt himself regaining control. At one time he had felt disastrously that he was losing it.

What exactly was Lee playing at?

He walked towards the barrier and, once through, looked back, convinced that Lee would still be there, that enigmatic expression on her face, waving at him.

But she had gone, which made her previous behaviour seem stranger still.

Lee Wylde, he decided, turning reluctantly towards the departure lounge was a vamp, an added complication in his life as unexpected as it was unwelcome.

*   *   *

'Oh this is fun!' Lee cried, glancing sideways at Becky. 'Just us girls together.' She pursed her lips and put her foot hard down on the accelerator, throwing Becky forward sharply and making her grateful for her seat belt. She looked nervously at the driver beside her.

Lee had had her new car for about a week. Everyone around her in the office said she could talk about little else.

Becky had spent the week clearing her things, too busy to see Max off at the airport. Anyway he liked to drive himself, leaving his car so that he could speedily get back to London again on his return.

'I'm just longing to see Steethey again,' Lee shouted above the roar of the engine. 'It's a part of the world I could easily fall in love with.'

'Maybe you could get a house there?' Becky called back.

'Oh I won't be here long enough.'

'When are you returning to the States?'

'That's in the lap of the gods. I've got to get a lot of things sorted out. Maybe a year, but not long enough to buy a house.'

'You're always welcome to stay with us.' Becky felt that her reply was polite, mechanical, but Lee threw her a grateful glance.

'You're an angel, but don't forget you'll soon be married! I'm sure Max will want to keep you to himself.'

Becky didn't answer and moments later the small town, nestling so picturesquely on the slopes of the cliff, came in sight and Becky began giving Lee directions towards the Versey home.

* * *

Her parents seemed genuinely pleased to see Lee again. Lady Versey greeted her with a kiss and Sir John shook her warmly by the hand. Stone bounded up to her with joy, as though greeting an old friend, and Becky was conscious of a pang of jealousy which made her rather ashamed of herself. Why was it that Lee, who to all intents and purposes was charm itself, brought out the worst in her?

80

'I've put you in the same room as before,' Lady Versey addressed her guest. 'You liked it, didn't you, with the view of the bay?'

'Perfect,' Lee enthused. 'It's so *darling* of you to have me again, so soon.'

'You must come whenever you like.' Sir John seized her case and turned to mount the stairs, leaving Becky to carry up her own.

She felt extraordinariy small-minded as she followed her father and Lee up the stairs, small-minded and petty. Why was it that everyone who met Lee, including the dog, succumbed at once to her charms?

Yes, small-minded and petty she told herself reprovingly as she trailed after her father and Lee, who were chatting away nineteen to the dozen like old friends. Lee, mature, well groomed, the epitome of charm, a few years older than Becky; a divorcee who made heads turn.

A person less like herself it would be hard to imagine. How, therefore, had she let herself become entrapped by her, by others, to go out of her way to be nice to a woman who, she decided, if she were honest with herself, she didn't really like? Why, to please Max. Why else?

Ashamed of her thoughts Becky reached her room and went in, shutting the door thankfully behind her. She heard her father and Lee go into the room next door, the animated patter continuing unabated.

81

She threw her holdall on the bed and went over to the window, leaning heavily on the sill and looking out over the sea, that beautiful, blue expanse of ocean on which, even though the day was cold, there was a flotilla of small yachts returning towards the yacht club from a race, their sails gleaming in the soft light of the afternoon sun.

She and Lee had left London just after lunch to arrive in time for tea. The nights were drawing in now; winter would soon be upon them and the boats would mostly be laid up for the season.

Becky peered down but she knew she would be unable to see Henry's house. Or was she perhaps, to be truthful, merely looking for Henry, hoping that he would be trudging up the hill, as of old, to do a few odd jobs in the garden? She sighed. So many things had changed since she'd met Max. A way of life, people, friends, particularly old friends like Henry. She seemed to be alienated from them all. Gradually they would disappear, supplanted by a new type of jet-setter like Lee, people who lived in the fast lane, utterly alien to her former existence.

Returning to her bed she apathetically unzipped the holdall and prepared to unpack the few things she'd brought with her. It was really an overnight case, as she left a complete wardrobe down here to change into.

Very soon now it would not be her room, her

den, hers alone. It would be *theirs*. Everything she had would be shared. Max would be in every part of her life. What was now just hers would be so no longer.

Was she being very selfish? Becky slumped face-down on the bed and stared at the floor. Love, after all, was about sharing, was a commitment to another person. And what if there were babies? There would be. If she was married she would want children, and that changed everything for good. Nothing ever the same again.

Maybe it was she who was the small child, afraid to grow up? In the next room Lee and her father were still chatting away and then, from downstairs, came her mother's call.

'Anyone for tea?'

Almost immediately the party that had gone upstairs converged on the landing again. Becky, her father and Lee, the latter still engaged in animated discussion, trooped downstairs where tea had been temptingly set out on small tables in the drawing room in front of a cosy fire.

Lady Versey was already pouring. 'The nights are drawing in aren't they? I'm glad you got here early. Do sit down Lee. Do you take milk and sugar? I should have remembered but I'm afraid I don't.'

'Yes please Margaret.' Lee, attractive in a slate blue trouser suit with a white cotton polo-necked sweater under her jacket, sat forward on the edge of her seat, hands clasped loosely in her lap, feet neatly tucked under her, the epitome of controlled emotion, sophistication and chic.

'Becky?' her mother looked over to her. 'You're very quiet. Is everything all right darling?'

'Everything's fine,' Becky said. 'I guess I'm just tired, Mummy.'

'She's been working terribly hard,' Lee intervened with a sympathetic smile. 'She has a lot to do getting things wound up before she leaves, and then there is all the excitement of the wedding! Not very long now.' She gave Becky an arch look which made Becky feel, at that moment, that she could have hit her.

'Have you actually done anything yet about preparations?' Her father walked towards her, stirring his tea.

'What sort of preparations, Daddy?'

'Well have you started to think about your trousseau?'

'Trousseau?' Becky looked puzzled.

'Oh *Becky*,' her mother laughed fondly. 'You're always so laid-back, darling. Don't pretend. You know perfectly well what a trousseau is. The clothes you wear for going away and on your honeymoon.'

'Oh Mummy, all that sort of thing went out with the Ark,' Becky protested derisively. 'I shall just be slopping around in jeans, and so will Max.'

84

'Have you decided where you're going for your honeymoon?' Lee's tone again was slightly superior.

'Haven't given it a thought,' Becky idly selected a sandwich from a plate near her.

Lee appeared to be about to say something, but hesitated, looking from John to Margaret, who imperceptibly shook her head. An awkward silence hung in the air, as though there was an unspoken question that nobody liked to ask.

*   *   *

After tea Becky tried to make up for what she knew were her bad manners, even truculence, and suggested a stroll. She wanted to smell the sea close to and feel the wind in her hair. Lee immediately agreed to join her while John and Margaret declined. They set off with Stone, promising to be back before dark and, Becky slightly ahead, made their way briskly down the hill.

'I thought we might pop in and say hello to Henry,' Becky ventured, slowing down while Lee, slightly out of breath, caught up with her.

'Oh I'd love to meet Henry. The mysterious Henry.'

'He's not mysterious at all.' Becky's tone was brusque, sharp, rather as she'd answered questions about her wedding.

'Well Max seems rather jealous of him.'

'Max despises him.'

'Oh?' Lee looked immediately intrigued. 'Why?'

'Because he's poor, has no proper job and smokes a pipe.'

Lee burst out laughing.

'Oh dear. That, if I may say so, sounds rather an attractive combination.'

'He's not a go-getter like Max. He's not really ambitious and he doesn't care a hoot about money.'

'He sounds rather nice.'

'Well, you'll soon find out.'

Having reached the bottom of the cliff, Becky led the way along the path towards the cottage which lay tucked away at the side of the bay. It appeared deserted and Becky's first thought was that Henry was out.

She knocked but there was no answer and, with a shrug and a glance at Lee, who was standing expectantly behind her, she was about to suggest that they resumed their walk when a light came on in the front room and a second later the door opened and Henry, wearing glasses, peered out. His expression of slight irritation turned to one of pleasure when he saw Becky.

'Oh hi,' he said, standing back. 'You're home again? Come in.'

'Have we disturbed you? Were you working?'

'We?' Henry glanced behind her and saw

86

Lee who stepped out of the shadows, hand outstretched.

'May I introduce Lee Wylde,' Becky said. 'Er, she's a . . .'

'Friend,' Lee said crisply, obviously to forestall being referred to as Becky and Max's boss.

'And this is Henry.'

'How do you do?' Lee said in that gracious, almost regal, manner which at the same time seemed to flatter and patronise those at whom it was aimed. 'I've heard such a lot about you, Henry.'

'Have you?' Henry looked amused. 'And *I've* heard a lot about you.'

'Really?' Lee was nothing if not direct and gazed at him appraisingly. 'Well I just love visiting here with Becky and Max. Becky's parents are so warm and charming with me.' Lee looked with interest round his cosy sitting room. 'And I hear you write?'

'Yes.'

'And also sail?'

'Yes, do you like sailing?'

'Love it.'

'I thought . . .' Henry looked from Lee to Becky, who had settled herself on the sofa and, her hand on Stone's head, was gazing out of the window.

'It's Max who doesn't like sailing,' she said without looking round.

'I have a boat on Nantucket Sound or,

rather, my father has.'

'Well you're very welcome to come out with us any time you want. Have you had tea by the way? I was just thinking of making a cup.'

'I'm sure we've disturbed your work.' Lee got restlessly to her feet, looking again appraisingly round the snug sitting room with its worn but comfortable furniture. Suddenly she seemed to be the one in charge while Becky looked on. 'No we had tea in the house, thank you Henry. We just wanted to take a walk, clear our heads of the dreadful London pollution, but as for your offer of sailing I'd love to take it up some time.'

'How about this weekend?' Henry glanced from Lee to Becky as if wondering why she was so silent.

'Isn't it a little cold?' Lee, pulling her warm, fashionable fake fur closer around her, gave a realistic shudder.

'Oh we sail all winter don't we Becky, weather permitting? As long as it's not too rough.'

Becky nodded.

'Well, maybe tomorrow.' Lee looked doubtful. '*If* it's fine.'

* * *

The following morning Lee appeared at breakfast in a tracksuit, white socks and white trainers. Becky was already downstairs helping herself to cereal and Sir John, reading the Sunday paper, looked at their guest in some amazement.

'You're going jogging Lee?'

'Sailing, John. Henry offered to take me.'

'Oh, you like sailing?' John chuckled as he put the paper back on the table. 'You'll be popular here. Becky's mad about it.'

'But not Max I understand?'

'Max isn't keen. I offered to buy them a yacht for a wedding present.'

'And he refused.' Lee popped two pieces of bread into the toaster and poured herself fresh orange juice. Margaret always had breakfast in bed.

'Pointless getting a boat if Max won't sail.' Becky poured milk over her cornflakes.

'Then what will you get them?' Lee addressed her remark to John.

'Well, maybe a house.'

'A house? How marvellous.'

'There's a house along the cliff I know Becky is keen on, but Max,' Sir John sighed deeply, 'Max doesn't really want to live here, does he darling?'

'Max wants somewhere nearer London.'

'That I can understand,' Lee said cautiously. 'But for weekends, here would be marvellous.' She gazed towards the window. 'Do you think Henry meant it about sailing?'

'Oh I'm sure he did. If you don't mind I'll pass. I want to work on my painting.'

'Oh but I can't go without you!'

'Yes you can. Henry won't mind at all. It's important to me to finish it. The nearer the wedding the less time I have for idle pursuits.'

'Of course!' Lee gave an understanding smile. 'As long as Henry doesn't mind.'

'Oh Henry won't mind,' Sir John echoed Becky. 'Henry is a *most* accommodating fellow.'

*   *   *

Later, Becky stood in front of her easel putting the finishing touches to the picture, maybe the last one she would paint of the bay before the hectic preparations began for the wedding. She kept an eye on the dinghy far out at sea, Henry's red sails clearly visible on the smooth surface of the water. Then acting on sheer impulse she painted it into the picture and, as she did, she tried to imagine their conversation and also desperately attempted to fathom her motives as to why she'd been so curiously eager to leave them alone together. She loved sailing; the picture wasn't important. Just a few hours of going over the brushwork and it would be finished.

Was she trying to discover if Henry was as fascinated by Lee's charms as Max? Was she trying to throw both the men she cared about into her path?

Cared? Did she *really* care about Henry, care

in the way she cared about Max? Was it possible to love two men in entirely different ways?

There was a soft knock on the door and she went to open it. Her mother stood outside with the coffee on a tray.

'Daddy's gone to play golf. I thought it was time for a break.'

'Lovely, Mummy.' Becky sniffed the aroma and stood back.

'Oh you've *finished*,' Margaret exclaimed eyeing the easel as she set the tray down. 'You've added something.' She went over and carefully inspected the canvas.

Becky raised an arm towards the sea.

'Oh how clever. You've painted in the boat,' her mother said.

'I thought I'd give it as a present to Lee.'

'What a nice idea, darling.' Margaret Versey took her cup and sat down, aware of her daughter's restlessness as she stood gazing out of the window at the boat across the bay. 'I really thought you weren't terribly fond of Lee?'

'Is it so obvious?' Becky said without turning round.

'I'm afraid so, but then I'm your mother.'

'I hope it's not obvious to her. Max'll kill me.'

'It's important to him of course.' Margaret paused as she sipped her coffee. 'Is it really *that* important?'

91

'It seems so.'

'Well I like her, I really do,' Margaret said diplomatically, 'and I think you disguise your feelings very well. I think giving her the picture will be a very nice gesture, and Max will be so pleased.' Margaret finished her coffee and sat back in her chair. 'Just think, in a couple of months you'll be married, and there's still *so* much to do.'

* * *

'I just don't know *how* to thank you,' Lee said, looking at the picture. 'With the boat in it, what a perfectly lovely idea.' She leaned forward to kiss Becky and for a moment the two women rather awkwardly clasped each other. 'And I *love* your studio,' Lee continued, looking round. 'What a perfect view.' She gazed out of the window and then turned to Becky, who was surprised to see on her face an expression of sadness.

'You're very blessed,' Lee said, taking a seat in the chair Margaret had occupied that morning, 'very lucky. You're so gifted, everyone seems to love you.'

'Everyone?' Becky looked nonplussed.

'Henry seems awfully fond of you. He talked about you all the time. Well, *almost* all the time.'

'We're all very fond of Henry,' Becky said with studied casualness. 'He's an old family friend.'

'Max *adores* you,' Lee went on as though she hadn't heard, 'and all your friends in the agency are desolate that you're going.'

She rose and walked restlessly across the room, paused and came back again as though she were counting the paces.

'I myself am not so blessed.'

'Oh but people admire—'

'Admire is one thing, love is another. I was married to a man who never loved me.'

'I'm sorry.'

'He also was an ad man and married me because of who I was ... Daryl Peake's daughter. He had ambition and wanted to make his way in the agency. Of course I didn't realise it at the time because I was so in love with him. He was very smooth, had enormous charm, but I was only a step up in his ambition. He had a mistress practically all the time we were married. I remained, and remain, unloved.'

'I'm *terribly* sorry,' Becky said. 'I really don't know what to say. I thought men admired you so much. Max ...'

'Oh men *admire* me but usually for what they can get. Of course I'm extremely fond of Max, but does he really like me, or is he trying to please me because of who I am, what I represent?'

'I ...' Becky felt words were suddenly inadequate. 'I think he ... both ...' she finished in a burst of candour. 'I think he genuinely likes you, admires you and, of course, wants to seem hospitable because, as you say, you are who you are. You're always going to have that Lee, as long as you are a powerful woman in business. If you want to know, I *have* felt very jealous of you. Max seemed to like you so much. You were everything I wasn't: soignée, beautiful, sophisticated.'

'Oh!' With that little self-satisfied smile Lee dropped on to the seat again and, producing an enamelled case from her bag, lit a cigarette.

'You don't mind do you?'

'Smoke away.' Becky placed an ashtray by her side. 'I don't, but I don't mind if you do.'

'I only do it when I'm tense or nervous.' Lee blew out the match and put it in the ashtray. 'And I feel both now. I did detect some hostility in you, and I didn't know why. I couldn't *imagine* that you'd think Max, who loved you so much, could entertain any feelings of romance for me.'

'Well I did. When I saw you at the terminal I was conscious of a feeling I'd never had before, and that was ugly jealousy. People at work pointed out how much time you and he spent together.'

'Oh can't people be vile? Of *course* we are together! *And* I suppose someone told you that I drove him to the airport. It meant nothing . . .'

'You drove him to the *aiport*?' Becky realised that her words emerged almost as an undignified squeak as she fought for control of her emotions.

'Oh didn't you know?' Lee hurriedly waved away the thin curtain of smoke between them. 'I shouldn't have mentioned it. I was only trying out my new car.'

'But Max likes to drive himself, so that he can get back without someone meeting him. I offered, but he specifically told me he didn't want me to.'

'That's what he told me. But I was crazy to try the car out on a bit of straight road. You know how it is? Really Becky it didn't mean a thing . . .'

'Max told me he was driving himself.'

'He *was*. At the last minute my car had just been delivered. I was dying to get into it.' Abruptly Lee rose and, going over to Becky, leaned towards her, peering anxiously into her face. 'Becky? Don't be a silly goose. Don't forget Max is my deputy. If we were going to do anything together—anything underhand, that is—and believe me we are not, you don't need to drive to the airport to do it. You must banish from your mind any feeling of jealousy. Please. Jealousy is such a destructive and senseless emotion.'

Briefly Lee let her hand rest on top of Becky's head, and then she turned and resumed her seat, the spiral of cigarette smoke still curling above her head.

Solemnly for a moment Becky looked at her. It was true that jealousy was a destructive emotion, but was it also senseless? Why had Max lied to her, and why had Lee brought up the fact that she had driven him to the airport?

'I'm sorry,' Becky lowered her eyes and shook her head. 'It's just that I felt a bit confused. Max told me he was driving himself and then you tell me you saw him off. I just thought it strange. Awfully strange.'

'But now you realise it was perfectly natural? Because of the car?'

'I suppose so. Yes I must believe you.' Becky raised her head, her eyes meeting Lee's. 'It's just that it made me feel insecure, anxious. I know I lack sophistication. I'm a simple person. I like painting and sailing, walking with the dog and running about in jeans. I don't want to live in Marlow or Maidenhead and entertain Max's business friends, run coffee mornings and talk to lots of stupid women.'

'But you do *love* Max?' Lee enquired tentatively.

'Oh I do . . .' Becky insisted, 'but I can't help thinking how much more suitable for him someone like you would be, rather than me.'

Lee sat there smoking thoughtfully, digesting what Becky had just said.

'I know what you mean,' she ventured at last, carefully stubbing out her cigarette. 'And I acknowledge that you have a point. The real point, however, is that Max loves you, not me. But even then I think your marriage may head for the rocks unless you do become more like me. This may seem a very strange thing to say, and I don't want you to misunderstand me.'

Lee rose and walking across the room put her hands solemnly on Becky's shoulders.

'I know what sort of person you are, and that's what Max loves in you. You're unconventional, carefree. Incidentally you're also beautiful. But I've noticed how often you and Max disagree when you're together. Little things, but they grate. One thinks "Uh-uh what's going to happen here?" You're artistic, casual. Max is ambitious; he aims for the top. He's going to be very very successful and, yes, he does need someone like me by his side; but that person is not me, but you.

'You, Becky, are going to have to change if you love Max enough, if you want to give him a chance to make the success of his life that he so yearns for. Believe me, any help I can give you I will. You can count on me as a very real friend.'

And once again she leaned forward to give Becky a warm, sisterly hug.

*   *   *

Lee left before nightfall taking her car. She and Becky had driven down together, but Becky said she'd take the train back, probably the following morning. They all had tea in the drawing room and then there were fulsome farewells. They watched Lee depart, taking her picture with her.

In a strange way the house seemed empty without Lee and Becky decided to go for a good long walk with Stone, to try and blow away all the dilemmas that Lee's visit and her conversation with her had so blatantly exposed.

She reached the bottom of the cliff path but, instead of walking along the beach, she headed towards Henry's cottage because she felt in need of a friend.

He seemed indeed surprised to see her but didn't hide his pleasure as he ushered her in.

'I hope I didn't disturb you,' Becky said apologetically.

'Not at all. Not at all. Come in. Tea?'

'We had tea,' she replied, 'just before Lee left.'

'Oh she's gone?' There was an odd sort of smile on Henry's face.

'She's gone.' Becky scrutinised his face. 'What did you make of her?'

Henry scratched his rumpled mop of hair. 'Honestly? I like her. I think she's a good sport.'

'Does she sail well?'

'She's very competent. She hasn't been in a boat for a long time, but she's okay. She was *very* kind about you. Likes you *very* much. Genuinely so, Becky.'

98

Becky thought back to her conversation with Lee, still undecided as to what to make of it.

'She told me I should change.' She bent to stroke Stone who, evidently deprived of a good walk, had lain disconsolately on the rug in front of the fire staring at Sandy. The days were drawing in and it was getting cold. Autumn was coming.

'Change?' Henry looked over at her.

'Become more like her; smart and sophisticated, so as to be a good wife to Max.'

Henry, aware of the irony in her voice, grunted but said nothing.

'I gave her a picture,' Becky went on, 'I'd painted in your dinghy when you were sailing and she looked pleased.'

'That was very nice of you. I think she's a strange, rather vulnerable woman, putting on an act.'

'She was unhappily married. Said her husband never loved her.'

'Maybe that explains it.'

'Funny thing,' Becky shrugged, 'I don't feel so jealous of her now, I guess because I know she's not invincible.'

'And *are* you going to change?'

'I'm going to try. I want to be a credit to Max.'

She rose, looking at the clock. 'I'd better get back or Mummy will worry.'

Henry looked out of the window and saw the gathering dusk. 'Shall I see you to your gate?'

'There's no need. Thanks all the same.'

'When are you going back to London?'

'Probably tomorrow. Lee went off this afternoon but I said I had things to do. I'm on part-time anyway at the office.'

'I shall miss you,' Henry said, accompanying her to the door. 'I feel like this is the beginning of the end.'

'How do you mean?' Becky turned to him in alarm.

'That I really and truly am losing you.'

She touched his hand but made no reply and calling to Stone set off briskly along the shore towards the cliff path while Henry remained where he was, staring wistfully after them.

However, there was still some daylight and Becky decided on an impulse to go further along the beach to give Stone the walk she'd promised him.

Turning to wave she found that Henry had closed the door maybe thinking that, having reached the path, she would continue up it.

She suddenly felt sad, vulnerable and alone. Not loved, not desired, not the sort of person Lee thought she was at all; young, rather small, as though she were once again a little child. It was absurd, of course, but she couldn't help the way she felt.

Ahead of her Stone bounded along the beach, stopping now and then for Becky to throw a pebble or a piece of driftwood. The sun sank slowly below the horizon. Night was setting in. Eventually she whistled to Stone and turned back, aware of the warm, welcoming lights in Henry's cottage. It looked like a beacon, but, tempting though it was to run towards it, it was one that she must ignore. Henry would always be there, or she thought he would always be there; the same kind, thoughtful, understanding person. A man who offered her comfort and love ... not conflict and passion, as Max did.

And who was to say she was making the right choice?

CHAPTER SIX

The model, slim, elegant, in many ways not unlike Becky to look at with blue eyes and bright gold hair, slunk along the catwalk turning first this way then that, showing off the designer suit she was modelling. It had no lapels, a short jacket and a thigh-length skirt. It was of very fine worsted, a subtle heather mixture, and the price tag was about £2,500. Becky had seen it once and had asked to see it again. If she was forced to buy *couture* she might as well have something she liked.

Beside her Lee's attractive mouth was creased in a grimace as the model stood waiting for instructions.

'I really *do* prefer the blue Chanel,' Lee said with an apologetic smile at Becky.

'Yes, but for you not me.'

'No, for *you*. It brings out the colour of your eyes.'

'And *yours*,' Becky smiled at her.

'True.' Lee wriggled uncomfortably. 'However, we're not buying clothes for me dear, but for you. I have two wardrobes full of suits.' An admission which did not in the least surprise Becky.

'Anyway it's terribly expensive,' she whispered.

'Hang the expense,' Lee whispered back. 'Regard it as business.'

Everything to Lee in the end came down to business. Next to them the head *vendeuse* pondered.

'What do *you* think?' Becky asked her.

'I think madam should have that in which she feels most happy and comfortable.'

'I feel comfortable in that suit,' Becky said firmly, pointing at the catwalk. The *vendeuse* made a note in her book.

'*Bien*. I will book madam in for a fitting. Now for evening . . .' She clapped her hands, the model disappeared, the lights were dimmed and a parade began of beautiful evening dresses, long and short.

They were staying at the Plaza Athénée in the Avenue Montaigne, where most of the top *couture* houses were. They must have visited a dozen of them, appointments made in advance by Lee's secretary. At the last moment Lee had decided to come herself for a few days in the French capital. It was, she told Becky, an excuse for a break, a brief holiday; but Becky thought it was more likely to make sure that she bought what Lee thought suitable. Maybe she was being unkind anyway, but it was not much fun being alone in Paris.

The wedding was now fixed for the end of January. The days were spent frantically attending the *maisons de couture*, the evenings dining at L'Ambroisie in the Place des Vosges or Les Ambassadeurs in the Hotel Crillon.

Lee certainly knew her Paris.

'I was a student here,' she explained to Becky after an exhausting day which had resulted in the purchase of two dresses for wear during the day, the suit which Lee didn't like, and a short evening dress which she did. In addition there were visits to the Rue de Rivoli and the Rue Royale to buy handbags, shoes and gloves. 'I didn't live like this though.' She held up her glass of champagne towards Becky.

'Here's to you, and Max and your happiness.'

'I can't thank you enough for what you're doing,' Becky toasted her in reply. 'Only . . .'

'Only what?' Lee's eyes twinkled.

'Only it all seems, well, most extravagant.'

'My dear it's an investment. As the wife of the boss we can't have you letting the side down. You'll have to do a lot of entertaining for Max you know. How are your culinary skills?'

Lee saw the look of doubt on Becky's face.

'Oh not too hot eh? Never mind, you can always get in caterers. Now . . .' she opened her filofax at a page full of notes, 'now tomorrow we have Versace and Lacroix, then the plane home.'

'Don't you think we have enough? Versace . . . he's so *terribly* expensive. And Lacroix . . . some of his fashions are outrageous.'

'Now then,' Lee raised an admonitory finger, 'I told you *not* to think about expense. I want to launch you, show you off. I thought Versace might do the wedding dress, or shall we choose the people who made the trousseau for the Princess of Wales? No!' She shook her head. 'One tends to forget how long ago that was, or what has happened since.'

'There's a very good little woman in Steethey,' Becky said with a mischievous smile. 'She would run me up something very fetching.'

'You're *teasing* me aren't you, Becky?' Lee reached over and pretended to tap her hand. 'You must be *very* serious about this my dear. It's not impossible that in a few years Max will be sent to the States, groomed to take over.'

'From your father?' Becky gasped as Lee nodded.

'My father is getting on.'

'But you?'

'Oh I will remain, of course, as president or something but I like my work as creative director. As we expand into different countries—and we have a full programme for expansion—I would like to travel more. Max is so wonderful at detail and organising. Believe me if you do come to the States we are talking about a very big profile indeed, for you, as well as your husband.' As Becky didn't reply, Lee put her head on one side. 'Penny for them?'

'I never thought it would be like this.'

'But you must have known that Max was ambitious?' There was a note of reproach in her voice.

'That was part of his appeal. I'm more laid-back. In many ways I'm rather a simple person, Lee.'

'Oh you're not simple, don't be ridiculous.'

'I don't mean simple-stupid. But I have simple tastes. Maybe that appealed to Max. I'm very different from him.'

'Opposites *are* often attracted,' Lee said lightly, beckoning to the waiter. 'I just want to make sure you don't bring Max down. Max must have a woman in every way worthy of him.'

*   *   *

At that point, thankfully, the waiter had intervened and Becky, who had been on the point of walking out, decided to simmer down and stay. Besides it would have caused endless trouble. Maybe by being so provocative that's what Lee wanted to do. She was a strange, enigmatic woman—her motives were difficult to fathom.

Instead Becky sat there agitated while Lee discussed the menu with the waiter in excellent French and in the end ordered a meal which was unsurpassable: *Ecrivisses à la crème* followed by *Canard aux olives* and chocolate tart to finish. The wine, about which Lee appeared as knowledgeable as she was about everything else, was a fine white Burgundy.

The meal left Becky feeling replete, impressed, but more inadequate—if that were possible—than ever. And now she lay in her sumptuous bed in the beautiful room at the fashionable hotel, unable to sleep.

Lee despised her, that was quite clear. A 'woman worthy of Max' indeed! Her cheeks flushed at the very recollection of the insult. That was the point at which she should have walked out but didn't. That was the moment of no return. Was she a coward, or had she done the right, sensible thing? She'd never know.

But the fact was that she had acquiesced in Lee's opinion of her by staying silent, and now she realised that in fact ever since they'd met Lee had patronised her, while pretending to be her friend.

Oh Max! How she yearned for him to make her feel self-confident again. She pressed her head into the pillow, imagining he was there beside her.

*   *   *

'Tell me about Paris.'

'It was fantastic.'

'Lee said you bought a lot of clothes.'

'Oh, you already spoke to her?'

'I spoke to her several times. She said you have a terrific figure for *couture*. I'm dying to see them. Best of all, though . . .' his eyes travelled the length of her naked body beside him in bed, 'I like you like this.'

'Oh Max!' She twined her arms round him and kissed him. They had fallen into bed as soon as she arrived. Her cases, still unpacked, remained in the sitting room. She seemed to need him to touch her, feel her, reassure her. By being good in bed she was proving that she was the equal of Lee.

But was she? She realised that she was beginning a new period in her life with Max: living a lie; pretending to like someone she not only disliked but was beginning to fear, in order to please him. By behaving like this she was stripping away, one by one, the real layers of her own true personality.

'Hey sex starved!' Max said, gratified, after he had returned her embrace. 'I can see you got up to nothing in Paris.'

'Of course we didn't get up to anything in Paris.' She released his body and lay on her back, arms behind her head. 'You don't think Lee, my chaperone, would allow anything like *that*?'

'Uh-uh!' Max glanced at the clock on the

bedside table. 'Don't tell me, here we go again. I thought you were good friends?' There was an edge to his voice. 'Lee said to me she thought you were.'

'As long as I do what I'm told.'

'Oh Becky!' Max gesticulated angrily. 'Don't be so unreasonable, ungrateful. Why, Lee gave up two days to be with you in Paris. She said you bought some fabulous outfits.'

'At fabulous prices. God knows how we can afford them. *I* certainly can't.' Becky ran her hands through her tangled hair, sat up and put her arms round her knees. 'Frankly, Max, I'm terrified.'

'Terrified?' He looked genuinely shocked.

'I'm terrified I'm going to let you down. Lee said that I had to be 'worthy of you'! Did you ever hear anything like it? I nearly stormed out of the restaurant.'

'Well thank God you didn't.' He sighed with relief. 'After all she did. I'm sure she didn't mean what you thought she meant.' He put an arm tightly round her waist. 'Lee means well, darling, she really does. It gives her a kick to see you buy nice things, take you to good restaurants.'

'It feels as though she's my keeper.'

'She's not your keeper! But she *is* grooming you. She's very experienced in a way you aren't. It's not *your* fault. I suppose you know they think in five years or so, maybe less, I'll take over from the old man himself. We'll have a penthouse in Manhattan, a country place in Maine . . . The agency is going to be one of the biggest in the world with billings of billions of dollars. Offices in New York, London, Paris, Rome, Vienna, Madrid. The European Union is going to offer fantastic opportunities, and there I'll be, right at the top. And if I am, Becky, with you by my side as I want you to be, in many ways we'll have Lee to thank for it.'

'Because she likes you?'

'She appreciates me,' Max nodded. 'Not in the way you think—not sexually—but for what I am, what I can do. She's a very powerful woman, and going out of her way to be helpful . . .'

'Like driving you to the airport,' Becky said accusingly, aware of how quickly desire faded and jealousy took its place. Max, normally so sure of himself, was taken off guard.

'Who told you that?'

'She did.'

'She just *told* you she'd taken me to the airport? I don't believe it. Someone else told you.'

'Oh, so then it was meant to be a secret?'

'Certainly not. But I know that you're jealous of Lee, unreasonably so in my opinion, and I'd prefer it if you hadn't known because, of course, you'd jump to the wrong conclusions.'

'She said something about trying out her car.'

'That was exactly it. It had just been delivered. She was as excited as a schoolgirl. I was about to leave and she said: "Why don't I drive you to the airport?" Of course, as you know, I prefer to drive myself, but because of who she is . . .'

'And who *you* are. Look Max, I think Lee is after you. She keeps on telling me what an effort I must make to be worthy of you, the sort of wife you need for success in your business career. In other words the sort of woman like her. All the time we were in Paris I was conscious of my inferiority. She knows all about *haute couture*, food, wine. Naturally she speaks perfect French. You'd think that being your wife was some sort of appendage. If anything is guaranteed to dent a girl's morale, this is it. Frankly I wish Lee had never come and now that she's here the sooner she goes back to the States, as far as I'm concerned, the better.'

*   *   *

'I'm so grateful for what you're doing for Becky.'

Lee collected her papers together on the desk and flashed a smile at Max.

'It's a pleasure. I'm so glad I went with her to Paris. She'd have been completely lost without me.'

'Oh she would.' Max also gathered his papers but remained sitting at the boardroom table where a planning meeting had just finished, deep in thought. It was the first chance he'd had to talk to her alone. 'It was good of you to take the time off to go with her.'

'I assure you it was no trouble at all. It was fun to have a few days away from the office. And you coped terribly well without me.'

Max had been left in charge. The first time, too, that he'd acted as head of the agency. Had she done it deliberately to see how he coped? But then, with his experience as Deputy, he knew he could cope very well. He was just raring for the chance to do it on his own.

There was, in fact, something vaguely patronising in Lee's suggestion that he'd done well in her absence. He felt that it was even possible that he was more experienced in the business than she was.

They reached the door in silence and he stood aside to let her pass. Because of Lee's passion for detail the meeting had gone on late and the building was now deserted. Lee and Max made their way, still in silence, towards the main hall where Joe, the porter, greeted them with a smile.

'You're the only ones left. Working late tonight?'

'Goodness,' Lee glanced at the clock in the hall which showed a few minutes to eight. 'Is it as late as that?'

'Afraid so.' Max stood aside again to let her pass.

111

'I do hope I haven't kept you Max? I feel very guilty about the others as well. You hadn't a date or anything?'

'No. Becky's in the country. I was going home to do some more work, as a matter of fact.'

Max reached his car which was parked near the entrance to the building and felt for his keys.

Lee stood beside him.

'I don't suppose you could run me home could you? I could get a taxi, but . . .' She let the words trail in the air.

'Your car out of order?'

'Oh just some slight adjustment to the steering. Nothing serious. I should have asked Joe to call a taxi for me.' She looked vaguely, and not very convincingly, towards the building they had just left.

'It's no trouble at all,' Max said smoothly. In fact St John's Wood, where Lee had her apartment, was en route to his own home in Hampstead. He opened the doors and then rounded the car to help Lee into her seat. She smiled at him gratefully.

'I hope I'm not taking you out of your way?'

'You know you're not.' Max looked rather pointedly at her and, closing the door on her, went round and got into the driver's seat. He switched on the engine, let in the clutch and the car purred smoothly away.

'I think the meeting went well.' Lee seemed

to relax and settled comfortably into her seat.

'Very well.'

'I like the new visualiser. The one who's taken Becky's place.'

'He's very good.'

'Not as good as Becky.'

'Different.'

'She has quite a career ahead of her as a serious artist, don't you think Max?'

'I do.' Max decided to cut through the park, and turned off the Marylebone Road. Traffic, now that the rush hour was over, was sparse.

'Will you let her continue with her career if she wants to?'

'Oh no question.' Max slowed down to suit the speed limit imposed in the park. 'But I don't think she wants to continue in commercial work. I think she'd like to concentrate on painting.'

'And you don't mind?'

'My dear,' Max looked askance at her in the light from the dashboard, 'these are the nineteen nineties. I don't think there is any question but that Becky will do as she wants to do. Not what I want her to do.'

'It's all very well saying that. But having a career wouldn't fit in with being the wife of a successful tycoon would it? I mean if you go to the States . . .'

'If Becky is keen to pursue her career as an artist she can do it anywhere.'

'True.'

Max crossed the bridge over the gleaming waters of the Regent's canal and drew up outside the block where Lee had her rented apartment. That too had an expanse of water in front of it from which a fountain sent kaleidoscopic, brightly coloured jets of foam cascading into the air. Soft lights illuminated the marble walls of the interior hall, the thick shag pile carpet, the golden lift gates. A uniformed porter hovered by the door ready to open it, an obsequious smile on his face.

'Would you like to come in for a drink?'

'I think . . .'

'Just a quick one. I shan't keep you from your work. I've got a lot to do too.'

Was there a note of mockery in her voice? Max wasn't sure. An invitation from Lee was in the nature of a command. Anyway, Max was rather curious to see what sort of place she had in this sumptuous block.

'Well just a quickie,' he said.

'Oh good.'

Lee looked up as the porter emerged and opened the door.

'Good evening Mrs Wylde.'

'Good evening Paul. Would you take Mr Lavery's car into the garage?'

'I shan't be long,' Max called, getting his briefcase from the back seat and handing Lee hers. Whereas his was bulging with papers he intended to work on, hers was very slim. The porter took his place behind the wheel and

Max followed Lee into the building. As if from an unseen command the doors of the lift slid open and, as they closed again, Lee pressed a button and glanced sideways at Max. Max, clutching his briefcase, stared in front of him feeling uncomfortable, unsure whether this was a wise move or, perhaps, a very foolish one.

Lee occupied the penthouse on the top floor of the building. From the windows of its enormous lounge there was a spectacular view across London.

She threw her briefcase on one of the two massive sofas covered in soft cream leather and went immediately to a table on which was an imposing array of drinks.

'I forget, what is your poison?' she asked, turning round.

'Malt Scotch would be very nice.'

There was the sound of a stopper being taken out of a decanter, liquid splashing into a glass, the clink of ice and then Lee came over to Max with the cut glass tumbler in one hand, the soda siphon in the other.

'Scotch it is. I hope you like it.'

'I'm sure I shall.' Max waved aside the soda siphon and appreciatively lifted the glass towards the light to admire the rich, amber colour, then put it to his lips. Lee watched him anxiously.

'Is it okay?'

'It's superb.' He put the glass down and smiled at her reassuringly. 'What are you drinking?' he asked.

'Oh Vodka and T for me. I have a couple at night and that's it.'

She went back to the table and began to pour while Max watched her. She wore a beige suit with a brown blouse underneath and a single row of pearls round her throat. Her hair, the style of which often varied, was today in a large, false chignon. She turned to him and smiled, her glass clasped between very long fingers, the nails blood red. The gentle, almost noble swell of her bosom accentuated the perfect cut of her jacket and he realised yet again that she was a very stylish, very attractive, very alluring, but slightly alarming woman indeed.

As she sat next to him he swallowed hard, aware that he was subtly, but inexorably being drawn into a trap.

'It's a beautiful place,' Max said, looking round at the huge room.

'It is lovely isn't it?' Lee crossed one leg over the other and he was conscious of her elegant limbs encased in sheer nylon, her soft brown calf shoes with a high, but not too high, heel. Everything about her was in perfect taste, and everything she did seemed to be done with this effect in mind. He drew his eyes away from her legs and looked into her eyes, conscious of the fact that she was observing the nuances of every expression, every gesture he made.

'Isn't it too big for you?'

116

'Well it is large, but I fell in love with it. Of course I have guests. Daddy will come over from time to time and the firm pays for it, so it doesn't matter whether it's small or large as long as I like it.'

'Quite.' Max paused, realising that he knew absolutely nothing about her. Their meetings, both in London and New York had always been professional, impersonal. There was always that air of self-containment, of unapproachability which was Lee. In many ways it was fascinating, and he realised that for quite a long time it had rather fascinated and intrigued him while he was, to all intents and purposes, in love with another woman whom he was actively courting. In less than three months' time he was to be married. 'Have you brothers and sisters?' he asked after a while.

Lee shook her head. 'Alas, an only child and I know I'm like one too. Spoiled. My mother died in a riding accident when I was six years old and I became the centre of my father's universe. You?'

'I've got two elder sisters. I suppose I was spoiled too, as my mother was also widowed when I was quite young and I became the man of the family.'

'Strange,' Lee murmured.

'Strange what?'

'We have never discussed anything personal before have we?'

He shook his head knowing that the almost

117

claustrophobic air of intimacy was increasing. He also knew that if you invited a member of your staff, who was of the opposite sex, back for drinks in your private apartment it was surely with the object of getting to know him better.

'You have,' she paused interrogatively, 'a house, an apartment?'

'I have an apartment in a house. It's one of those large, old Victorian villas in Hampstead converted into flats. Mine is on the second floor and I have a nice view of the Heath.' He swallowed some more whisky, aware that his mouth was drying up; his tongue felt leathery.

Lee carefully put her glass down on the long, low table in front of them and uncrossed her legs. Then she rose and, arms akimbo, walked restlessly to the window and remained there for some time gazing out over the city.

'My apartment in New York overlooks Central Park. Then there is the family house in Nantucket Sound, but you know Max,' she swung round and gazed at him, one hand playing with the pearls at her throat, the other clasped under her arm, 'it is still possible to be lonely even if you are surrounded by luxury.'

'Oh, I know.'

'Some people think I have everything and in many ways I do. Everything that money can buy. Many people, I know, consider me hard.'

'Oh no.' Max protested gallantly.

'Oh yes.' She came back slowly into the room and resumed her seat beside him. 'They think

I'm hard and bossy and domineering. I try not to be but, in a way, I can't help it. It doesn't mean I'm less of a woman, less of a real person for all that.'

'Of course it doesn't.'

'Now your little Becky,' Lee took a sip from her glass and carefully replaced it on the table, 'she is a complete contrast to me isn't she?'

'I suppose she is.' Max was aware that her tone, as well as her manner, had once again become slightly patronising: 'little' Becky. Well Becky wasn't little at all. If anything she was taller than Lee who was trying nevertheless to diminish her in Max's eyes.

'I took her over, carried her off to Paris, bullied her into buying clothes she didn't want, just because *I* felt she should have them.'

'Oh I wouldn't say that,' Max protested, feeling increasingly ill at ease, obsequious like the porter downstairs, wishing that there was a way of escape, looking at the door, tightly shut. 'She was very grateful for what you did.'

'No she was intimidated by me. She always has been. Come on Max, you know that. Don't pretend.'

'Becky was certainly jealous of you.' Max finished the drink in his glass which he held up. 'May I have another?'

'You certainly may.' Lee gestured towards the drinks table, 'Go on, help yourself.'

'Will you?' He held out his hand.

Lee touched the top of her glass and shook

119

her head. 'In a moment. I haven't quite finished.'

Max took his time pouring his drink, noting that the whisky was a very fine, very expensive brand of the best Scotch malt. He raised the decanter to his nose and inhaled appreciatively.

'Like it?'

He turned, surprised by the proximity of her voice and saw that she was standing next to him, very close, gazing up at him. Just then she seemed invested with an ethereal glow, with the allure, the physical attraction of a woman who had somehow metamorphosed into the essential mystery of femininity. He felt an overwhelming sensation of raw desire as though someone had spiked his drink, yet he knew it wasn't the drink, nor was he drunk. It was her.

And he knew then that he had been resisting her for a very long time.

He put down the decanter and, as he turned to her again, her arms reached out for him and seemed to envelop him in an all consuming, all powerful, irresistible embrace.

CHAPTER SEVEN

Sir John Versey was a rich man, a generous man and he loved his only daughter. He wanted her to do well and to be happy and he thought that in Max she had found the perfect partner.

Sir John was a handsome man in his early fifties who kept himself in good trim with exercise and golf. He had a power boat in Majorca and went there several times a year. He had long ago given up sailing, which he left to his son and daughter, but in his youth he had been almost Olympic class. This was the first time for many weeks that the family had been at home together. Miles, as the sales director for the business, was frequently away.

Miles was two years older than Becky but whereas she was fair, he was dark: brown hair, brown eyes. They didn't look like brother and sister. Miles was mercurial with a very low boredom threshold. He liked Max and got on with him. Now he sat in a chair listening to his father's comments as he turned over the brochures of country houses which Max and Becky had been inspecting without coming to any firm conclusion about which one they preferred.

Miles had a girlfriend, was contemplating marriage himself, but was in no hurry. Let Becky get her nuptials out of the way. Besides, his intended bride was a girl he had known most of his life and she was unlikely to run away.

'Well!' Sir John finished examining the house particulars and then put them on a table and glanced up at Becky. 'They're all pretty pricey, darling. Prices are supposed to be coming down, but I see no sign of it here.'

'At this level of the market they don't Father,' Miles said laconically. 'Heated indoor swimming pools and the rest.'

'Half a million! It's a lot of money.' Sir John whistled.

'Daddy, I certainly don't want you to buy anything at this level,' Becky said heatedly. 'I didn't ask you to. I'm simply showing you the sort of thing that Max . . . and Lee expect.'

'Why do you say "Lee" in such a bitter tone darling?' Her mother, who had also been listening, butted in. 'I thought you liked her better? She's been awfully kind to you.'

'She's grooming me to be fit to be Max's wife, if you call that kind.'

'Oh come!' Sir John picked up one of the glossy brochures again which showed an ancestral pile on the Sussex/Kent borders with eight bedrooms, an indoor swimming pool and stables for horses. Maybe at one and a half million it was cheap at the price. 'Well, if I'd have bought a yacht it would have been a quarter of a million; even one from our yard. I daresay . . . ' He stroked his jaw.

'Daddy I think it's quite out of the question.' Becky jumped up and, snatching the brochure from her father's hand, added it to the others and swept them up into a pile. 'I'm sorry I showed them to you.'

'But I *asked*.'

'I feel ashamed,' she said. 'People are being thrown out of jobs, losing their houses, and we're contemplating spending on a massive scale like this. It's all so . . . *unreal*. The whole advertising world is unreal.'

Miles rose and moved restlessly to the window. Margaret picked up the paper and John sat where he was, fiddling with his hands. They were all shocked in their different ways by Becky's outburst. Margaret perhaps most of all because she suspected the depth of her daughter's unease and was upset by it. Were they so anxious for her to marry well that they hadn't stopped to wonder whether Max was the right man? On the other hand, they so liked him, and Becky, her mother was sure, loved him.

'At least you're having the wedding dress made here,' she said. 'You got your own way over that. You can't really blame them darling for wanting you to become accustomed to the style in which you're going to live.'

'I'm out of my depth,' Becky said wildly. 'I don't think I'm suited to it.'

'You're lacking confidence that's all it is.' Miles's expression was sympathetic.

'There's no reason why she should lack confidence,' his mother said. 'None at all. I call it pre-wedding nerves. We have always lived well. We have wanted for nothing.'

'Yes, but not on this scale,' Becky burst out. 'We spent a fortune in Paris, and that was not only on clothes. We travelled Club class and stayed at the best hotel, ate at the best

123

restaurants.'

'Go on, you enjoyed it,' Miles chaffed her. 'Lucky thing, I say.'

'It's not *me*.' Becky appeared more and more distressed. 'Don't you *see*? It's not *me*. I love Max. I adore him, but they're trying to make me into something I'm not.'

'Then you must be firm with them,' her mother said sharply. 'Tell them you want to be your own woman, as you did over the wedding dress, and wear what you want to wear.'

'And live where you want to live,' Miles put in. 'You love it here. Whiteways up the road is going for about £200,000, well under the cost of the yacht Dad had in mind. You could furnish it for another £100,000 . . .'

'Max doesn't want to live in Steethey. It's too far away.' Becky gritted her teeth.

'But for the weekends? It's only five miles from the motorway.' Her mother looked pained.

'I think he believes it's too provincial, frankly. He's set his heart on the Thames valley.'

'Well the Thames valley it is then.' Sir John bewilderingly scratched his head. 'I'll have to have a word with Max and see what we can do.'

'Oh Daddy!' Becky flung herself on her knees by the side of her father and rested her head in his lap. 'You're going to ruin yourself on our account. Please don't. Tell him you can't afford it. Make him realise what life is

124

really like . . . that it's not all fantasy from the advertising world, glamour, expense accounts and smart hotels . . .'

'Darling.' Sir John gently rested his hand on her head and stroked her hair. 'I can't tell him. If you feel that, you must tell him. After all . . .' he raised her chin with his finger and gazed into her eyes, his expression worried, 'you're the one who's going to marry him. You do still *want* that Becky don't you?'

Becky sat back on her knees and the gentle, loving, concerned expression on her father's face brought a lump to her throat.

'You see darling,' he continued, 'we don't want you to marry Max if it makes you unhappy.'

Her mother took off her reading spectacles and put the paper aside as though she'd been merely taking refuge behind it. 'We don't want you to marry him at all costs just because you've gone this far,' she said; 'it's not too late to back out.'

'I don't want to back out. I do love Max.' Becky's expression was now calm. 'I simply don't love all *this* . . .' she made a gesture of contempt towards the estate agents' brochures.

'But Max is that kind of man.' Miles went over to his sister's side, squatting beside her. 'Max likes glamour. You must have known that.'

'It sounds as if you've all got doubts,' Becky said.

125

'Because we think *you've* got doubts.' Her father leaned forward in his chair and gazed at her. 'We like Max very much. We were happy for you, and him; but you've never seemed very happy since you got engaged. Not *really* happy.'

'You seemed positively dismayed when we brought forward the date. That's what made us wonder,' her mother said. 'It's just that you haven't been yourself for a long time Becky, and we love you so much that we want you to be happy.'

'I think I'll go for a walk.' Becky got abruptly to her feet. At the sound of the magic word, Stone, his head resting on the hearthrug as though he had been taking in every word, got to his feet, tail wagging furiously.

'Shall I come with you?' Miles also rose.

'No, I want to have a think. Maybe I'll see what Henry says.'

'Henry!' her mother cried in alarm. 'Whatever has *Henry* got to do with it?'

'He's always been such a friend,' Becky replied. 'You're family, but he's a good, dispassionate friend.'

'As long as that's all he remains,' her father said grimly. 'For God's sake don't ever come back and tell us you're going to get married to Henry.'

'I'm not as a matter of fact,' Becky said coldly, 'but I *would* like to know why you're so against him?'

'Darling, if you're attracted to a man like

Max you can't possibly consider Henry.'

'I'm not.'

'That's good.' Her father gave a loud sigh of relief.

'But I *would* still like to know why you do consider him so unsuitable?'

Sir John waved a hand vaguely in the air as if at a loss for words.

'Familiarity breeds contempt,' Miles said after a while. 'I mean, I *like* Henry . . .'

'What you *mean* . . .' Becky had to choose her words carefully, 'is that Henry has no ambition. He is *not* a go-getter. Well as it happens I don't intend to marry him—as a matter of fact he's never asked me—but if I did I would find that a recommendation rather than a disadvantage. So there.'

And clicking her fingers for Stone she half walked, half ran out of the room.

* * *

It was true she was volatile, stormy. That's what Max had told her he loved about her. She seldom listened to reason, but followed her heart.

The pale wintry sun was low on the horizon but the whole bay was bathed in an evanescent glow and as soon as she got back to the house she resolved to try and recapture it on canvas. It was a glorious sight, almost like a painting by Monet.

Henry would give her coffee. Henry would talk quiet, good sense and, restored, she would wander back to the house and immerse herself in her work. Her spirits raised, she threw a piece of driftwood as far out to sea as she could and watched while Stone went pelting after it. Then she threw another and another, and thus got nearer and nearer to Henry's cottage.

Really, going to Henry was like coming home; the old dear, familiar face of her old, dear familiar friend.

Eventually she and Stone stood on the steps of Henry's cottage panting with the exertion of the exercise. Instinctively Becky tried the handle first but the door was locked. She felt a sharp pang of disappointment, but nevertheless she knocked on it. She thought she heard a noise inside, listened and knocked once more.

'Who is it?'

'Becky,' she replied, puzzled at this very un-Henry-like behaviour.

'Oh Becky!' Henry pulled back the bolt and opened the door. 'Sorry.'

'Sorry?' She gazed into the room which seemed very gloomy after the bright morning outside.

'It's just that I'm working. Well . . .' he pointed to a chair in the corner. 'Meet Susan Chiltern, my literary agent.'

'Hi!' A hand was languidly raised from the depths of the chair by the fire and stretched out towards hers. Limp fingers clutched hers. In

128

the chair sat a woman of about thirty, attractive rather than beautiful with sharp, intelligent features. She had rather untidy brown hair which looked as though it hadn't been combed that morning. Susan wore a thick brown sweater and jeans; she had no make-up on and could, in fact, just have got out of bed.

Becky gazed at her with shock as the implication of what she was thinking dawned on her. It was a strangely intimate atmosphere and she felt like an intruder.

'Hi!' she said, shaking the hand. 'Sorry to burst in.'

'That's perfectly all right. Henry was just about to make us some coffee.'

The 'us' sounded so familiar and personal, as did the way Henry turned cheerfully into the kitchen after murmuring 'Shan't be a mo.' They couldn't have known each other long, yet sounded like old friends. Very close old friends.

Could it be . . . was it possible that he and Susan were *lovers*?

Why not? She and Max were. Why shouldn't Henry have a lover too? Or was it simply that, in her heart of hearts, she thought he loved her and should kick his heels waiting . . . waiting and waiting for her to make up her mind.

When you came to think about it, she had a bit of a nerve.

She looked round for tell-tale signs. On the table in the middle of the room were the pages of a typescript. Henry had obviously been sitting there while Susan sprawled in the chair, doing what? Listening? Discussing? Becky knew nothing about how people wrote books and Henry had always been curiously secretive about his hobby. Or rather up to now it had been a hobby, and how much everyone, except her, had scoffed at it!

'So what do you do?' Susan asked conversationally once Max had left the room.

'She's an artist,' he called out. 'A very good one.'

'Oh?' Susan's rather world-weary expression grew more interested. 'Successful?'

'Commercially yes. Until a few weeks ago I worked for M, M & P.'

'Don't know them I'm afraid.'

'Meredith, Maidstone and Peake, the advertising agency.'

'Oh yes, I have heard of them. Up to a few weeks ago?'

'She's marrying the boss.' Henry kicked wide open the door as he brought in two mugs of coffee and put one before Becky and the other in front of Susan. 'Quite soon now Becky eh?'

'January,' Becky said woodenly.

'How exciting.'

Susan didn't, in fact, look at all excited. If anything she appeared bored, one of those people on whom it was difficult to make an impact. They could be rather trying at times.

'Tell me . . .' Becky turned her attention to Henry, who had now returned with his own coffee, closed the door and taken a place at the table. 'Has your novel been *accepted*?'

'Not yet,' Susan replied for him. 'But it will be soon. I'm very excited by it. We're just working on a few suggestions I made and then, hey presto! Fame!' She flourished her hand in the direction of Henry who made an elaborate bow.

Looking at his face Becky thought she had never seen him so animated. Gone was the air of indolence, the laconic expression, the composure, the pretence at boredom. Instead his eyes blazed with excitement and his body seemed taut with vitality.

Was it love, or the excitement about his book? Hard to tell.

'Well I'm delighted,' she said. 'Thrilled for you, Henry.'

'It hasn't happened yet,' Henry said cautiously, but his happiness bubbled through. 'Thanks to you in a way, Becky.'

'Me?' Becky looked surprised.

'It was your friend Ruth at your engagement party . . .'

'Of course.'

'Oh *that's* who you are.' Susan finally showed a glimmer of animation. 'I know who you are now. The girl next door. Henry's always talking about you.'

'I am not "always" talking about her,' Henry said indignantly. 'On the contrary . . .'

'Becky this, Becky that. She sails, she paints,

131

she's beautiful and yes, I must give it to you but . . .' she wagged a roguish finger at him, 'funny you didn't *also* tell me she was engaged to be married to another man.'

'Henry and I are just very old friends,' Becky said swallowing hard. 'We have known each other almost all our lives. You can admire someone without being involved with them. Can't you Henry?'

Henry didn't answer and, seemingly embarrassed by the exchange, was busy riffling through the pages of his typescript as though trying to put them in some kind of order.

Susan raised her hands above her head, stretched, gave a deep yawn and then jumped up energetically from her chair.

'I must be off,' she said. 'I have an editorial conference this afternoon and I want to tell them how good your book is and how it's coming on.'

'Well thanks for all your help.'

'Look I'd better go,' Becky began awkwardly.

'No you stay,' Henry said quickly, 'I'll just go and see Susan off.'

'Nice to meet you.' Susan perfunctorily held out a hand.

'And you.' Becky replied politely taking her hand and shaking it.

'You keep an eye on Henry,' Susan said with a wink. 'One day he's going to be a famous man. Remember you heard it here first.'

Becky stood by the window watching Henry see Susan to a smart little car that had been parked outside the cottage. They stood for a long time, apparently deep in conversation, heads rather close together, and then they both simultaneously burst out laughing at something. Susan then leaned forward while Henry pecked her on the cheek and, still chuckling over whatever it was that had amused them, opened the door by the driver's seat for her to get in.

Even then they hadn't finished. Susan, hands on the wheel, was saying something else, and Henry's face was almost touching hers as he bent forward to listen. Finally he stepped back. A roar came from the car's twin exhausts, and with a wave Susan was gone, while Henry stood for a long time gazing after her.

'Well!' Henry came back into the cottage face aglow, looking pleased. 'That was a very successful visit.'

'Good.' Becky sounded laconic. 'She seemed nice.'

'She is, and a very good editor. She took endless trouble with the book and had obviously done a lot of work beforehand.'

'How long had she been here?' Becky pretended casualness.

'A couple of days.'

'That long?'

Henry studied the ceiling as if doing a mental calculation. 'She came on Tuesday, today is Thursday. We started work Tuesday afternoon and finished this morning, say a day and a half.'

'Did she, er . . .' Becky looked enquiringly around. 'Did she stay here?'

'At the pub.' Henry returned to his typescript which was flagged with coloured markers. 'We ate there last night, both nights in fact. She paid or rather, I suppose, her agency did. It's rather nice being a kept man.'

'I can imagine.'

'Becky.' Henry leaned forward and looked at her closely. 'Is there something bugging you?'

'Nothing.' Becky ran a finger along the table. 'Nothing at all.'

'Don't tell me you're jealous, Becks?'

'Of course I'm not jealous!' she exclaimed indignantly. 'I'd be very happy for you, Henry, if you found a nice woman to settle down with. After all, I shan't be around long. It would be selfish of me to wish you anything else but happiness. And, sincerely, I do.'

Henry's mouth set in a thin line and, wandering back to the table on which his typescript reposed, he put on his spectacles and began idly flicking over the pages, as though his mind had gone back to his work.

'Was there something you wanted particularly, Becky?' he asked without looking up.

'Just a chat,' she said, rapidly swallowing the rest of her coffee. Then she rose, putting the

134

cup on the nearby table. 'Just now it doesn't really seem the time or place.'

'I can see you're annoyed about something.' Henry removed his glasses and putting his hands in his pockets in a casual, rather indifferent sort of gesture, stood there gazing at her.

'I'm not annoyed at all.' She sounded defiant.

'Maybe it was seeing Susan here?'

'That's *rubbish*. I told you I'd be very happy for you . . .'

'And I'm very happy for you,' Henry said rather pointedly, 'to have found a nice, steady, successful man like Max to share your life with. Consequently if I should achieve any literary success—and there's no certainty that I shall— I hope you'd be similarly happy for me.'

'Of course I would. You know that.'

'Perhaps if I was successful you'd reconsider your relationship with Max?'

'What on earth do you mean?'

'Come on, isn't it because he regards me as a bit of a drifter that your father so much prefers Max to me?'

'Daddy's got *nothing* to do with it,' Becky said hotly.

'Oh I think he has.'

'Well you're wrong, he hasn't.'

'I'm not the right sort. Don't tell me he hasn't influenced you in all this?'

'No he has not!' Becky felt her face flame

135

and she turned abruptly towards the door, flicking her fingers for Stone to follow her. Reluctantly he heaved himself up from his comfortable place by the fire and did as his mistress commanded.

'I don't believe a sensible girl like you would fall for a bounder like Max unless your old man had something to do with it.'

'Frankly I hate you, Henry Lamb.' Becky cried over her shoulder. 'Max is worth *ten* of you.'

And she tripped, almost fell, out of the door and rushed across to the beach pursued by a galloping Stone.

Henry walked slowly to the door and stood at the threshold watching her until she disappeared into the mist rising from the sea. Then thoughtfully, sadly, he closed the door.

He'd gone too far, he was sure of that. By rudeness he'd turned her against him, perhaps irrevocably. But he'd felt desperate.

He sighed. Was it now, after all, really too late?

CHAPTER EIGHT

The animated presentation, cartoon-style, was amusing, entertaining. The animators had done their job well and the presentation was informative as well as interesting. The packet soup was full of natural goodness: organic vegetables, animals raised in a natural habitat; happy bullocks, contented pigs, free range hens, herbs, and so on, completely free of additives, of course. All the animals were shown trotting obediently, all the vegetables and inanimate substances flowed into the packet from which the ensuing liquid poured into large, prettily decorated earthenware bowls. The family sang a catchy jingle over the bubbling broth, emanating a wholesome feeling of wellbeing.

The clients were delighted. As the lights went up there was a chorus of approval. Lee, sitting between the managing director of Supasoop and Max, promptly turned and called to Becky at the back, sitting with her colleagues, but no longer feeling one of them. They wore jeans and T-shirts, she wore a navy dress with red collar and cuffs, tights, shoes with neat heels, Italian, bought in Paris. She'd come straight from the hairdresser, Gilles of Bond Street. She no longer felt part of the team and sat on the edge of the group, already an outsider. As Lee turned towards her it seemed inevitable that they would all react as they did: sullenly, unsmiling, suspecting her of favouritism.

'And this is Rebecca Versey,' Lee announced, 'We call her Becky. She was the visualiser who worked on the initial drawings.'

The managing director swooped towards her. 'You did a great job, Becky. We like your work very much. Perhaps you can work for us again?'

'Well . . .' Becky glanced diffidently at Lee.

'Becky is marrying our acting Managing Director, Max, in January,' Lee said enthusiastically, propelling her forward, 'but we hope to persuade her to act for us in a freelance capacity. I'm sure she'd be happy to continue with the account, wouldn't you Becky?'

Becky was aware of her erstwhile colleagues in the background beginning to drift away, exchanging meaningful glances in her direction. Her heart sank.

'Well . . .' she glanced at Sarah who lingered by the door, 'I don't *really* want to take work from my colleagues who are here full-time.'

A spasm of irritation crossed Lee's face.

'That's not a very helpful attitude, Becky. After all, if it's your work they want . . .'

'I'm quite sure Becky will cooperate.' Max put a hand on her arm. 'We all want to keep our clients happy.'

'We do hope you will.' Mr Supasoop put out a hand. 'And we wish you every happiness in your marriage, Miss Versey.'

'Thank you. Now, if you don't mind . . .' Becky signalled urgently to Sarah and, with a smile at Lee and the client, squeezed Max's hand and murmured, 'See you later.' Then she ran after Sarah.

'What an ordeal,' she said, grasping her

138

hand.

'It's an ordeal I wouldn't mind,' Sarah replied, looking at her enviously. 'Everything's going your way at the moment, Becky. Here there's a rumour they're sacking half the art department.'

'Oh no!'

'Lee was really brought in to cut costs. Billings are down.'

'But Max never said anything. I was told we were expanding.'

'That's what they like us to think.' As they reached the door of the office they used to share Sarah stood back for Becky to precede her. 'Probably that's why they got rid of you, flattering you to think you were being groomed to be Max's wife.' Her eyes lit up maliciously. 'Maybe *Max* will be without a job. Who knows?'

'I can't believe it.' Becky slumped at her former desk, now empty. She began to think that perhaps she was the victim of some sort of conspiracy. 'We seem to be doing so well don't we? I mean, despite everything. You really think that's why Lee came over?'

'So they say. I only hear rumours.' Sarah paused and Becky found her gaze unnerving. 'So, how are plans going for the wedding? You've changed Becky. I hardly recognised you when you came in.'

'Well we're going to look at some houses.' Becky glanced down at herself apologetically.

'Then there's some dinner or other tonight, I think with the soup people and some other clients. I . . . I'm still a jeans and T-shirt girl Sarah, believe me. Every day of my life I dress as I've always dressed. Inside I'm the same too.' She gazed at her earnestly.

'But for how long?' Sarah's eyes looked sad. 'For how long can you stand the pressure?'

*   *   *

Becky felt like a nervous schoolgirl waiting for a sticky interview with the Head as she stood in front of Lee's door and, after a few moments, gave a timid knock. There was no reply and she knocked again, glancing sideways at Lee's secretary, Jean, who had told her she was in. Jean gave an affirmative nod.

'Come in,' Lee called at last and Becky pushed open the door and peered round.

'Only me,' she said.

'Becky!' Lee rose from her desk and, with an apparent exclamation of pleasure came towards her, hands outstretched.

'To what do I owe the pleasure?'

'I wondered if I could have a word?' Becky glanced past Lee to her neat desk, everything just so, not a paper or paperclip out of place, precise and tidy like Lee herself.

'Of course dear. Come and sit down.' Lee put an arm round her shoulders and drew her towards a long, low sofa that stood at the far end of the office and which, with a couple of armchairs, was used for informal meetings. In front was a glass table with an attractive arrangement of flowers in the centre, a couple of ashtrays, and a few up-to-the-minute magazines which carried ads produced by the agency.

Becky felt uncomfortable with Lee's arm round her, but it would have seemed rude to shrug it off. Yet, somehow, she resented this cloying *bonhomie* of the older woman. It seemed so false.

'Would you like coffee Becky?' Lee looked at her as, together, they sat down.

'No thanks. I have to meet Max and we're going to look at a house.'

'Say that's great. Where, may I ask?'

'Somewhere on the Thames. I'm not quite sure where. Max has seen it and is most enthusiastic.'

'You must feel very excited.'

'Yes.' Becky looked at her woodenly. 'Lee I've come to see you because I'm not very happy about this suggestion that came up this morning that I should remain working part time. I thought that you had replaced me, and that was that?'

Lee threw her arms upwards in a gesture of despair. 'My dear what can I do? You appear to be irreplaceable. Mr Supasoop likes you so much and, really, you *are* our best visualiser. The very best.'

141

'It's kind of you to say it, but I think that's an overstatement. Besides, I understand there are to be redundancies in the art department, and it doesn't seem fair to keep me on when I don't need work, and sack others who do.'

Lee reached out and touched her arm. 'Becky how sweet of you! How typical! Always thinking of others! I wish I had a nature as good and kind as yours.'

Was there a hint of mockery in her voice? Becky couldn't be sure. She felt again rather childlike, rather naïve under Lee's steady, unflinching gaze. At the same time she thought her—more so than ever—a duplicitous woman. Someone not to be trusted.

'But is it true?'

'Well,' Lee put her head on one side, 'there *may* be some reorganisation after Ted Levine goes—and we're working on putting an attractive package together in the hope of persuading him to leave early, incidentally. Though keep that to yourself.' She gave Becky a conspiratorial wink. 'Some tightening up. I think everyone expects things like this from time to time. It makes sense in the aftermath of a recession, even though we were not as badly hit as some of our rival agencies. I do think there is a weakness in the art department, and we would have been making changes there anyway. We can't just keep people on if they're not up to the mark, Becky. We're not a charity.'

'No, I didn't think you were.' Becky glanced

142

at her watch. 'But there are some very good people in the art department. Every bit as good as me. Frankly, Lee, I felt embarrassed this morning and I want to tell you now that I will not stay on part-time. Also if Max does become managing director I'd be in an invidious position. In fact from today, from this very moment, I don't intend taking on any further work for you again.'

'I see.' Lee looked at her coldly, her attitude completely different from that of a few moments before. 'That's your final word is it, Becky? Despite one of our most important clients wishing specifically to retain your services?'

'Yes, I'm afraid so.' Becky's resolute tone faltered and she hung her head. Put like that she suddenly felt rather mean.

'Of course you haven't had the chance to discuss this with Max have you Becky?'

'No.'

'Then I should, if I were you, and when you have come to some decision let me know and we'll talk again.'

'I have come to a decision,' Becky said. 'Whatever Max says, I have made up my mind.'

A spiteful gleam appeared in Lee's eyes. 'It won't make any impact on my decision to enforce redundancies. In fact, in view of what you say, I might conceivably bring them forward.'

'But why?' Becky looked at her aghast.

'Because we really do need first-rate artists, and we haven't got them. You, as it happens, *are* a first-rate artist and I'm not flattering you. I mean it. If you were on hand to help out, maybe I could keep on some of your less talented friends to do the donkey work.' Lee put a hand on Becky's arm, gave it a quick squeeze and then got up. 'Think about it. Now I'm afraid I have a meeting, and you mustn't keep Max waiting.' She frowned, 'Though come to think of it he should be here today. I know getting married is very exciting and all that, but I wish you could confine your house viewing to evenings and weekends. Max is an important member of the team, one we can hardly spare when serious decisions have to be taken.'

Becky also rose and looked at Lee who had returned to her desk as though she had already forgotten she was there and her mind had passed to the next item on the agenda.

'Max is OK, isn't he?'

Lee raised her head. 'OK? How do you mean?'

'Well I mean . . . his position here. I heard a whisper that redundancies were not to be confined merely to the art department.'

'Oh I see.' Lee gazed at Becky, her face lit by a mysterious and slightly menacing smile. 'No one is indispensable, dear. Not even me. Run along now like a good girl and enjoy yourself.'

Becky went to the door aware that the

feeling she'd had before the meeting had never really gone away—the feeling that she was a small, recalcitrant schoolgirl who had been given an equal dose of praise and blame by the headmistress.

She closed the door gently and, from her desk, Jean looked up and gave her a sympathetic smile.

*   *   *

The house was on the banks of the Thames, with beautiful lawns running down to the river and its own private mooring. It was on two floors and the master bedroom and two private suites each led on to a separate balcony.

On the lawn a giant weeping willow hung rather wistfully over an ornate pond stocked with fish. It was a cold, wintry scene, but a beautiful one.

Despite its architectural merits, its commanding position, its fine appointments, the house bore a look of neglect, as though it had long been empty. It was their second inspection and the estate agent, anxious to make a sale, had certainly been keen to impress them with its advantages.

'What happened to the last owners?' Becky asked as they stood in the drawing room looking out on to the lawn, still covered with a patina of the morning's frost, on which birds hopped up and down vainly looking for crumbs. There was a pregnant pause as the agent failed to reply, and Becky looked round. 'It has the feel of having been empty for ages. Did they go abroad?'

'Well, er . . .' the agent glanced nervously at the particulars he held in his hand. 'The house was the subject of a repossession order.'

'You mean the people were *evicted*?'

'I'm afraid so. Not *evicted*, as such, but they were unable to keep up their mortgage repayments.'

'I'm surprised that people like this had a mortgage.' Max was evidently as astonished by the news as Becky.

'Well they took out a mortgage when the owner fell into difficulties in his business. You know how it is.' The agent shrugged.

'What business was he in?' Becky's mouth felt dry.

'I'm afraid I'm not at liberty to divulge that information,' the agent said frostily. 'But of course the situation and circumstances are reflected in the price. All in all the house is in very good condition. You've got a bargain here.'

Becky shivered as suddenly the ghosts of the past occupants, people who had lost the home they loved, seemed to pass silently across the floor.

'Had they any children?' she asked, imagining the garden ringing to the sound of laughter.

'I . . . wouldn't really know.' The agent began to stammer. 'We're selling on the instructions of the bank. I know nothing about them.'

'Well we don't like the house,' Becky said firmly, 'do we Max?'

'I thought you did, darling?' He looked confused. '*I* think it's charming.'

'Well I don't.' Becky drew her coat firmly around her shoulders.

'Becky it's silly being sentimental. Thousands of people have had their homes repossessed.'

'That doesn't make it right.' Becky stubbornly pursed her mouth.

'Someone's got to live here.'

'But not us.'

Not only Max but the agent seemed annoyed too. 'I do think this is a *little* unreasonable, Miss Versey,' he said. 'This is a most desirable residence which someone will buy.'

'Let them then.' Becky turned to the door. 'But *I* have a conscience.'

The agent shrugged and ushered his clients through the hall and out of the front door, which he shut firmly behind him. Max stayed to shake hands with the agent and have a few words with him—she could only guess what *they* were—but Becky got straight into the car. When Max climbed in beside her she could tell he was livid.

'I'm sorry,' she said as he peremptorily turned the key in the engine.

147

'I don't think you're sorry at all!' he fumed.

'I am.'

'You're sorry for those wretched people, not for making a *fool* of me.'

'Max I did *not* make a fool of you.'

'Well I *felt* a fool. It is the second time I've seen the house. I even discussed an offer.'

'But we didn't know the circumstances.'

'Well next time . . .' he looked witheringly at her, 'please don't ask. That was a super house in a lovely position. It needed very little doing to it and the price was right.'

'I can't live where I know people were unhappy.'

'You don't *know* they were unhappy.' He put the car into gear and eased it along the long drive towards the imposing front gates.

'Of course they were unhappy. Wouldn't *you* be unhappy at losing your house?'

'Becky, I repeat, you don't know the circumstances. How can you be the judge? Honestly darling you're far too sensitive.' He stopped abruptly at the gates, looking to right and left. 'If you're going to ask about the circumstances of *everyone* who lived in every house we see we'll get nowhere. I'm very annoyed about it Becky. Very. I don't think your father will be too happy either.' He gave her a scathing look but she stared straight in front of her.

'Is it true half the art department is being sacked?' she asked.

'Why?'

'That's what I'm told.'

'Who by?'

'Never mind.'

'Sarah I bet. Well *she's* on the list and . . . yes, we are cutting down.'

'Sarah is on the list to be sacked?' Becky was shocked.

'Redundant I believe is the term.'

'But that's *awful*.'

'However,' he shrugged offhandedly, 'necessary, I'm afraid.'

'Was that why I was moved out?'

'You were not "moved out". You know perfectly well the motivation behind that. Besides I don't believe that whatever your situation you would have been on the redundancy list. You're too good and too valuable to the agency. You're a much, much better artist than Sarah. You undervalue yourself, Becky, really you do.'

'And what about you?'

'Me?'

'Are you being made redundant?'

He gave a short, mirthless laugh. 'Well I hope not, as I'm being groomed to take over from Ted.'

Suddenly an awful realisation struck Becky.

'Is *that* why Ted is on indefinite sick leave? He's been *sacked?*'

'Well you could call it something like that. Permanent sick leave, really.'

'That's monstrous!'

Max abruptly braked and brought the car to a halt. His hands gripped hard on the steering wheel and he stared in front of him, his brows drawn together as though he were trying hard to control himself.

'Becky, my dear girl. Seeing that you are disinclined to face reality let me spell it out for you. Ted Levine has not been a very good ad man, frankly. It's due partly to poor management that our billings are down. We need to progress from a position of strength and, to use one of your favourite nautical metaphors, to trim our sails. We did a lot of hard talking in New York and I was forced to agree with the conclusions that Daryl Peake and his senior colleagues came to. In order to succeed we have to be very fit. Lean and fit.'

'But those dresses and suits I bought,' Becky said furiously, 'they cost *thousands* of pounds.'

'We are talking about *millions*,' Max said laconically. 'A few thousands on dresses is neither here nor there. Besides, it is very important to keep up appearances, darling. We are *not* going down, but we mustn't even be *thought* to be going down. Fly the flag at all costs. Fly the flag. And you, as my wife, will help to keep it waving.'

Becky folded her hands on her lap, her mouth set in a stubborn line. 'I'm beginning to hate the whole of the advertising business. It's a racket. It's dishonest. Supasoop is a joke. I'm wasting my time and talent on such rubbish. And I told Lee this morning that I would not work for the agency again.'

'You did what?'

'At the presentation with Supasoop they were all over me. Lee said they wanted me to stay on and help with the campaign. Mr Supasoop himself wanted me. Then I heard—all right from Sarah—about the redundancies. I went and saw Lee and told her it was immoral. The whole thing was immoral...' She looked at Max, beginning to feel a little fearful. Maybe she had overstepped the mark? But he had lowered the window and, one elbow resting on it, was gazing over the tranquil landscape of the Thames valley, as though lost in thought. 'Are you listening to me Max?'

'Yes I'm listening.'

'Who does Lee think she is? That's what I want to know.'

'She's the daughter of the boss, that's who she is. A very powerful woman and also, incidentally, a very clever and successful one.'

'She makes me feel like a child. Frankly I dislike her more and more.' Becky paused, feeling her way. 'She more or less said your job was on the line too.'

Max removed his elbow from the window ledge.

'In what way exactly?' His tone was interrogative, as cold as Lee's had been when

Becky had told her that, quite definitely, she was leaving.

'She said no one was indispensable. Not even herself. I don't think she meant anything. Perhaps I shouldn't have asked.'

'You *asked* her if my job was on the line?' He sounded incredulous.

'In a way I suppose I did. I said I'd heard there were other redundancies. I think she was just being catty because she was annoyed with me.'

'Understandably annoyed I'd say.'

'She wasn't pleased you weren't at the office today, by the way.' Becky glanced at him slyly.

'I don't have to explain everything to Lee. Actually I was having a meeting with an important client at Claridges. I thought I was entitled to a few free hours later in the day if I wanted them.'

'She asked if we'd keep our house viewing hours to evenings and weekends.'

Becky realised she was beginning to enjoy herself. Too often she was the mouse, fearful, creeping into her little hole. Suddenly she felt more confident, powerful, independent—free.

'You *have* put your foot in it.' Max exclaimed and started the engine again putting his foot hard down on the accelerator before he released the brake, as if to emphasise his point, so that the car produced a mighty, deafening roar and jerked away at speed, in a reaction of his mood.

CHAPTER NINE

'She's a little mouse,' Lee said, leaning back on the pillow, hands behind her head.

There was silence from the man next to her. She turned her head and looked at him. He too was lying on his back, replete after lovemaking, but without a smile on his face and gazing at the ceiling.

'Max?'

'She's not a little mouse,' Max said without looking at her. 'She is a very thoughtful, caring, nice person.'

'Oh I agree.' Lee said quickly. 'Don't misunderstand me. She's a darling.'

'Then why are you calling her a mouse?'

'Because she is. Max, darling, she's not your sort. You must know that. I don't see how you can possibly go on with the idea of marrying her.' Lee sat up in bed and, groping for the packet on the table beside her, extracted a cigarette and lit it. Then she lay back again exhaling a thin stream of smoke into the air.

The conversation about Becky had begun over dinner in Lee's apartment; an intimate *dîner à deux,* not the first that had been held there since Max and Lee became lovers. It was judged to be wisest to eat at her place where they were unlikely to meet people they knew.

The conversation had almost turned into a row between them. Tempers had flared and it

153

ended as these things often do, when passions are raised, in bed.

Theirs was a very passionate relationship, the intensity of which had taken Max by surprise. It had also made him feel very guilty. Fancying a fling with Lee was one thing, getting involved with her was something else. It was very, very foolish and, he realised, a threat to his relationship, maybe his very future, with Becky.

'Is it the money?' Lee asked after a period during which Max had failed to reply.

'Money?' Stung, he looked at her.

'Her father's very wealthy I understand.'

'Of course it's not the money! I find that an insulting remark, frankly.'

'Sorry, I didn't mean it that way. But you're not exactly *flush*, are you Max? I mean I do know a little about your background. You have no inherited wealth and, as I understand it, no capital. I believe old Versey is a millionaire many times over.'

'You seem very well informed.' Max's tone was brittle.

'Well it's my job to know these things.'

'I can't see how John Versey's wealth affects *you*.' He stared accusingly at her.

'No but it affects *you*, and if we are considering someone for the top job we have to probe very carefully into their backgrounds. Can't afford to take chances.'

'I see. That sounds like a threat. Hardly

pillow talk is it?'

'Oh darling!' She hastily stubbed out her cigarette and, turning towards him, tried to put her arms around him. 'Don't you realise, Max, that I love you? I want you. *I* want you and I don't want Becky, or anyone else, to have you.'

Max tried to remain unresponsive to the sinuous movements of her body as she began to arouse him by entwining her legs around his. She was a very beautiful woman. Her body, golden brown, was almost perfect—well proportioned, with a full bosom and a flat stomach. She was not skinny and she was not Junoesque. She was very, very sexy and he controlled himself now with difficulty. But one thing helped. The word he had dreaded hearing: Love.

Impassive to her entreaties, verbal as well as physical, he gently detached himself from her and, sitting upright, looked at his watch. It was midnight. He felt extreme weariness.

'What happened with the house?' Lee, as if realising she had made a fool of herself, sounded composed.

'Becky didn't like it.'

'Oh? Why?'

'It had been repossessed.'

'So?'

'She thought it would be unhappy.'

'I see. She is a sensitive soul isn't she?'

'She is. Very. Lee . . .' Max turned towards her. 'This can't go on you know. I didn't mean it to . . .'

'You just wanted a fling, was that it?'

'No. I find you very attractive. I may be attracted to two women at once, or even three or four I suppose, but I can't love them all. I think I am in love with Becky.'

'You think! But you tell me you quarrel all the time. Disagree about almost everything. What kind of love do you call that?'

'I think we're a bit nervous. A bit tense. I expect it all to be ironed out after we're married.'

'I see. So you do intend to go ahead with it?'

'Yes. I do.'

'And you don't love me? At all?'

'I like you very very much. I respect you.'

'Respect!' Lee gave a harsh laugh. 'What use is respect? As a matter of fact I don't think you do respect me. A woman who throws herself at you. No restraint. I bet you think it's very flattering. I bet you think I'm an easy lay. Hungry for sex. Desperate for a man. I bet you despise me.'

'I don't think that at all, nor do I despise you. Quite the contrary. I wanted to sleep with you ever since I met you; but now everything has become more complicated. You are, after all, my boss. Becky's position in the organisation is very complex. I mean, you don't like her as a person and yet you think she's a bloody good artist, which she is.'

'I don't *dislike* her as a person.'

'Oh come. You're always putting her down. You lose no opportunity to denigrate her. 'Little' Becky when she's taller than you. 'Mouse' when she is anything but . . .'

'She *is* very timid, Max, I don't care what you say. She came creeping into my office today like a schoolgirl who'd committed a misdemeanour. I feel that you need someone more vigorous, spunkier. Someone like me. I'm much more your sort of woman, Max. *And* I would make it very worth your while. Daddy likes you. We don't just have in mind the managing directorship of the English organisation for you. We're considering the possibility of making you MD of the whole group, which will mean you need someone by your side who is worthy of you and, frankly Max, I don't think Becky is and nor, I'm sure, will Daddy.'

* * *

Max drove slowly home, up Avenue Road, through Swiss Cottage, along the Finchley Road until he took the turning off to his home in Hampstead.

He was in an awful situation. Lee had more or less thrown down the gauntlet. He must choose either her or Becky. His job might be on the line. He didn't know just what influence Lee had on her old man, or vice versa.

Besides, in many ways he thought Lee was

157

right. She was more suitable for him: tough, accomplished, streetwise. A woman who knew her way around. She loved parties, entertaining. She was articulate, knowledgeable, good at making people feel at ease.

And to be MD of the whole group! His mind catapulted at the thought.

On the other hand, the debit side—and it was a big debit—Lee was a bitch. She was hard and she frightened him. She mesmerised him too, but it was rather the attraction of someone for a snake, something sinister that, however beautiful, you could never trust.

Becky was the opposite. She had a fragility, an ethereal beauty that melted his rather hard, pragmatic heart. He knew he was selfish, spoiled, used to getting his own way. Becky gave in to him. Lee wouldn't. With Lee there would be fights galore, followed by a glorious tumble in bed. But how long would that last? Once passion was spent, what would happen then?

Becky seemed to retreat into her shell. She was shy. That's what made Lee unkindly call her mouse-like. But Becky wasn't a mouse, she was artistic and had the temperament to go with it.

Max knew he could certainly desire as many women as he liked, and he was that sort of man who liked women, to whom sex was important because as well as gratification it was also power. But could he actually love more than one?

He certainly knew he couldn't love Lee. You couldn't love a woman you feared. In time she would emasculate him, but if he was chairman of the company, would it matter?

Max drew up outside his house and sat for a while after he had switched off the engine and turned off the lights. He looked up at the house and saw, to his surprise, that a light was on in the front room on the second floor. His living room. Had he left it on in the morning? It had been dark when he'd gone to work.But then his cleaning lady had been in. Maybe she'd left it on?

An awful thought occurred to him and, collecting his brief-case he got quickly out of the car and locked it. Then he hurried through the gate, along the path and let himself into the hall. He inspected the table just inside the front door for post. There was nothing for him. His keys still in his hand, he went up the stairs two at a time and let himself into his flat.

He put his case down in the hall, examined his face briefly in the mirror, straightened his tie and gently pushed open the living room door.

Becky was fast asleep on the couch. She'd been reading and her book lay limply in one hand, against her chest. She had very long, beautiful eyelashes which on her closed eyes gave her a rather helpless, babes-in-the-wood

159

kind of expression. She looked very pale and vulnerable, like a child; so lovable. So very different from Lee.

He sat gingerly by her side and his fingers brushed her face. Her eyes flew open and she sat up in alarm, clutching at his hand. 'Oh it's you.' She flopped back on the couch.

'Who did you think it was?' His voice was very tender. He felt at that moment that he loved her so much and didn't want to lose her.

'Where have you been?' She rubbed her eyes and looked at the clock on the mantelpiece which was now ornamental, because it was many years since there'd been a fire.

'I had a meeting.' He shrugged and began to move away but Becky held on to his hand.

'Where?'

'In the City. With the clients I saw today. We had left a few things to finalise. It's been a hard day.' He crossed to a chair and sat down, rubbing his eyes. He was in fact extremely tired. Exhausted. Drained. If only it was just work that was difficult; but it was his trying emotional life as well.

'Poor darling.' Becky came over to him. He took her on to his knee and she leaned against him, his hand tight round her waist. She was so slight, a slip of a girl, featherlight.

'I felt awful about this afternoon,' Becky said, aware of the heavy beat of his heart against her breast. 'I couldn't settle. I rang you to suggest we had dinner together.'

160

'Couldn't make it.' He shook his head and ran a hand across his brow.

'I really think you work too hard.'

Guiltily, remembering the dinner at Lee's, the passionate sexual encounter that followed it, Max said nothing. What was there to say? 'I'm a liar and a cheat. I am not worthy to tread on the same ground as you'?

'Do you forgive me?'

'*I* forgive *you*?' Max looked at Becky, shaking his head. 'There is nothing to forgive. You're an angel and I can't wait to be married to you.'

'Do you really mean that Max?'

'Yes I do.'

'Because I wondered recently.'

'Why did you wonder, darling?' He stroked her hair back from her brow and looked longingly into her eyes.

'Well we've had so many, I won't say rows exactly, but misunderstandings. I mean like today and the house . . .'

'You were right. I mean apart from being repossessed there was something I didn't like about it.'

'But you said you loved it.'

'No.' He shook his head. 'It wasn't right. I don't quite know why, but thinking about it later I decided you were right. Darling,' he looked at her urgently, 'it's terribly late. Shall we . . .?'

*　　　　*　　　　*

Later, much later, Becky lay in the dark unable to sleep. The lovemaking had been awful. Catastrophic. Max had tried so hard, it had exhausted them both. He'd apologised, flopped on his back and explained that he was just terribly tired.

Of course Becky understood. She always did. She could find an explanation for everything, whether it was his attempt to rape her or his inability to make love to her. Both times she felt rejected and maybe it was a weakness, but she was so nice she couldn't help finding an explanation, an excuse for everything that affected someone else. She blamed herself for the failure. This time she had failed to stimulate him.

But there was something else. About his body there was an odour which she finally identified as tobacco. Max didn't smoke and yet there it was in his hair, on his skin, a very faint but unmistakable scent of stale cigarette smoke.

He'd spent the evening with clients. Maybe in a smoke-filled room? Could that be the explanation?

And then, in her mind's eye, she saw Lee sitting behind her desk, that Mona Lisa smile on her face, a long filter-tipped American cigarette between her fingers. For an American Lee was politically very incorrect about tobacco. She was quite a heavy smoker. She smoked at dinner. She smoked between courses, which Becky hated. Did she, perhaps, also smoke in bed? Becky immediately hated herself for the thought, the unworthy thought, that Max was Lee's lover as well as hers. She tried to banish it from her mind, but she was unsuccessful and lay awake in turmoil until well after dawn.

*   *   *

'Hi.' Lee gave Max a friendly wave and pointed to the sofa. 'How did it go?'

'What?'

'The dinner with Supasoop. Sorry I couldn't make it.'

Lee had been away from the office for a week. A board meeting at senior executive level had summoned her back to the States. She had only arrived at Heathrow early that morning and yet a few hours later she was her usual immaculately-groomed self, not a trace of jet lag.

'Oh it went well.'

'Did Becky go?'

'No. She couldn't make it either.'

'Oh.' Lee thoughtfully pursed her mouth and lit a cigarette. 'I suppose she was afraid of being persuaded to go on with the ad campaign against her will.'

'No. She was in the country, with her parents. She had to have fittings for her dress and is also looking at a couple of properties

163

down there.'

'I see.' Lee leaned forward and flicked her cigarette into the large circular ashtray.

Studying her slow, deliberate actions, wondering what cunning plans were formulating in her devious mind, Max realised he hadn't missed her at all. 'How was the board meeting?'

'Oh fine. Fine.' She turned and laid a hand lightly, yet possessively, on his arm. 'But good news Max. Great news. You *are* to be the new MD, Great Britain. It's confirmed. Immediate. However, Dad wants me to stay on a bit longer. I think he's keen for me to be sure that everything is settled once Ted has gone.'

'How long does your father want you to stay on?' Max asked.

'Oh, indefinitely you know.' Lee moved closer to him. 'He thinks we'll be a good team, you and I that is. I think I might start to look for a permanent property here. I believe there's another apartment going in the same block. Not as big, but certainly very spacious. As soon as I can get time to take a look at it I shall.'

'So, a very long time?'

'Aren't you pleased?'

'Lee you know I told you this has gone far enough. Between us.'

'I know you told me, darling, but I don't think you mean it.' Lee laid a hand firmly on his knee. He visualised her naked body, very brown from extensive use of the sun lamp, the tiny hairs on her stomach, blood red nails on the pillowcase. He swallowed. 'I do mean it Lee. I am going to marry Becky in a matter of weeks . . .'

'I feel I must prevent you committing a folly you will bitterly regret. I know you will Max. Becky is not for you. You simply aren't suited. Daddy, as a matter of fact, would like you over in the States right away. For an indefinite period. I also know that he would much prefer it if you were to arrive without a wife.'

Max rose and went to the window. There he remained for some time jiggling the loose change in his pocket. The office on London Wall overlooked ancient parts of the old City of London that had escaped the bombing. Not much of it left. A few bits of walls, bricks, stones, hallowed ground. Then there was the unsightly mass of the Barbican. The best thing to have done with that monstrous pile would have been to pull it down and start again. Why did people, even governments, city planners, get themselves into such messes? Make so many mistakes?

Why couldn't he have resisted the lure of the boss's daughter and not landed himself in the terrible predicament he was in now? Was it vanity? The knowledge that he could pull her if he wanted? It certainly wasn't frustration. He had a perfectly good sexual partner in Becky.

'Lee I want to hand in my resignation,' he said, continuing to gaze out of the window. 'I

165

know this just won't work.'

He turned to face her, but her head was bent as she busily lit a fresh cigarette. 'Don't be stupid,' she said finally, between puffs. 'Don't be so dramatic.' She flicked off her lighter, leaned back against the sofa and stared up at him. 'You are the man for this job and we want you. *I* want you but, most of all, Daddy wants you.'

'Does Daddy know about Becky?'

'He knows you are engaged.'

'You've talked about Becky with your father? Told him that she is a mouse, unsuited to be my wife and all the things you tell me?'

'Well . . . not in so many words. I did say that I thought she was too individualistic to fit into the mould of a corporate wife.'

'Oh really? Well that was nicely put. A step up from being a mouse.'

'Don't be sarcastic Max. You can't quite bring it off. I'm sorry if I offended you, but I do call a spade a spade and I couldn't resist being honest with you and telling you exactly what I thought. However . . .' She flicked ash into the tray again. 'We think far too highly of you to lose you. Also, quite honestly, I don't think you would so easily find elsewhere the kind of generous executive package we're going to offer you, to say nothing of the scope for self-fulfilment. I will not accept your resignation. I have no intention of it, and if Daddy heard about it he'd have a fit.'

'Does he know about us?'

'Oh no,' Lee vigorously shook her head. 'Daddy is a puritan. I think he knows that I like you, find you attractive and, as he likes you too, I think he'd be pleased if we . . . made a go of things. Okay, well, shall I fax Daddy that you'll come or not?'

'For how long?'

'Daddy thought about three months.'

'Impossible. Couldn't it wait until after the wedding? Either that, or a very brief visit . . .'

'And you won't resign?'

'I want to keep my options open.' Max busied himself collecting his papers, and then he rose and stood looking at her. 'Lee it *has* to be all over between us if I am to stay on here. I'm completely serious. I like you as a friend, want you as a friend, but I can't go on leading a double life. You've got to believe that I mean it.'

*   *   *

After Max had gone Lee stood for a long time in the same place as he had occupied by the window, looking out on to the ancient City ruins. There were tears in her eyes which she brushed impatiently aside. She was being weak, showing all those womanly attributes in herself which she despised in others. But hadn't she been weak, very weak about Max? Hadn't she shown how vulnerable her emotions were?

She had fancied Max Lavery from the moment she met him, some time ago now, in

167

New York. Her lousy marriage was behind her and a succession of brief, unsatisfactory flings had been followed by a period of stagnation, and frustration. There were too many gay men around in New York. Gay, or married and on the lookout for something that wouldn't last.

And then Max appeared—attractive, accomplished, sophisticated, good looking. Above all, virile. She had thought she detected a look of interest in his eyes, that certain *je ne sais quoi*, when he addressed her. But she had also thought it clever at first to play hard to get. And it was during that time, when she was busy being clever, instead of seizing her chance, that he got engaged to the little mouse.

Becky *was* a mouse. Tall she might be and beautiful but Lee liked, in her mind, to diminish her as a person who was mouse-like. It was an attitude rather than a physical thing. Someone she could dominate and, if possible, frighten. She felt she had partly succeeded, but the snag was that she had also managed to frighten Max too.

Too clever by half.

Lee had been quite determined to get Max once she knew he was spoken for, and she'd used a combination of sex and her power over him as his boss to do it. She had sussed him out quite well. She knew he was venal and also ambitious, unscrupulous and greedy; a lot like her. She was quite sure, once she had got him in bed, that she'd been successful. The little *dîners á deux* followed by a stormy session between the sheets had become a regular part of her lifestyle.

What she hadn't been able to bring herself to believe, and could barely credit, was the fact that he had fallen in love with the little mouse and intended to marry her, when he could have had Lee Wylde with all her gifts and wealth, her social attributes and fabulous connections, a lifestyle so many would have envied. And now he not only wanted to end it all but, possibly, leave the company too. What was more Lee felt he meant it. Somehow he had got the upper hand over her. Daddy would be furious if he thought she'd muffed it, lost the company he had built up from small beginnings a first-class executive. Daddy was the one man she really respected, admired—and was afraid of.

Lee adored Daryl Peake, who had been her lifeline since the early death of her mother. Everything about him she loved and admired. If only other men could be like Daddy: that insipid husband of hers, Mervyn Wylde, and dozens of others in between, before she met Max.

Max, she believed, was different. Max was much more like Daddy. And now the man after her own heart was proving elusive. More than that, she already felt she had lost him.

The tears were now rolling freely down Lee's cheeks and she brushed them angrily away again, cursing herself for being the sort of weak woman whom she so despised.

She blew her nose vigorously and went briskly back to her desk, picking up the telephone as she sat down and, after consulting her pad, dialled a number.

For some moments she listened impatiently, tapping her fingers on the desk while, at the other end, she could imagine the sound of the telephone echoing through the house. Maybe Becky was at her easel, reluctant to answer, while her mother was out shopping, or otherwise engaged.

Finally the ringing tone stopped and a voice said a crisp 'Hello?'

'Hello Margaret! Is that you?'

'Yes.' A pause, then an expression of pleasure. 'Why Lee! How nice to hear from you. How are you?'

'I'm fine and you?'

'Oh fine, fine.'

'Busy I guess. Eh?'

'Oh very busy.'

'Is Becky at home by any chance, Margaret?'

'Yes, she's right at my elbow. I think she thought you might be Max.'

'Sorry to disappoint her.'

'No, she'll be pleased to talk to you.'

Lee could hear Margaret Versey murmuring to her daughter and then Becky's pleasant voice at the other end said, 'Hello Lee. How are you?'

'Fine. Just fine. Look Becky, dear, I wonder

170

if it would be too much trouble for you to pop up to London to see me? I'd like to take you to lunch and choose your wedding present. Maybe at Harrods? Are you coming up any day this week by any chance?'

'Well,' Becky sounded dubious, 'it's awfully nice of you, but . . .'

'It's not just a social invitation. There's something quite important I want to ask you.'

'Is it about work? Because I've said—'

'No it's not about work, well not about you.'

It was about Max! Fear clutched at Becky's heart and, wide-eyed, she stared at her mother.

'Okay. What day would you like Lee?'

'Is Thursday all right? Could you make it for lunch at San Lorenzo, say one o'clock? Is that okay?'

'That's fine.' Becky replied. 'See you then.' Slowly, thoughtfully, she replaced the receiver as she turned to her mother who was gazing anxiously at her.

'Is everything all right, darling?'

'I hope so,' Becky replied. 'I think it may be about Max. I simply don't trust that woman at all.'

*   *   *

San Lorenzo was the sort of smart Knightsbridge restaurant famed not only for the quality of its food but as a place where people went to see and be seen. Lee liked it

171

because it was trendy; she liked being seen there and also enjoyed seeing other important and celebrated people she knew.

She found Becky already seated when she arrived and apologised profusely for keeping her waiting.

Becky appeared at ease and was sipping mineral water with ice and lemon. She greeted Lee, who bent to kiss her cheek effusively, with a smile. 'Hi!'

'Hi Becky.' Lee sat down, looking round the crowded room to see if there was anyone she knew. A few tables away sat a man and a woman, heads close together. The man saw Lee, looked up and waved. Lee waved back and turned to Becky with a knowing expression on her face.

'That's Gerald Bates the TV presenter. *And* the woman with him is not his wife!'

'Maybe just a friend? Possibly a client?' Becky suggested, but Lee sniggered in a rather unpleasant, knowing kind of way.

'Success has gone to that man's head,' she said as the waiter arrived with the menus, presenting one to Lee, the other to Becky. 'Have anything you like,' Lee said airily. 'This is a celebration.'

Becky wasn't hungry. She felt nervous and apprehensive. Despite her friendly air, her unctuous manner, Lee suddenly seemed an overpowering, menacing kind of presence with the power over her and Max of life and death. How could she ever have attempted to like a woman like this, never mind trust her?

Lee was unconcernedly nibbling a breadstick and looking at the menu. 'The veal is divine here,' she said.

'I'd just like smoked salmon, please.' Becky put the menu back on the table.

'As a starter. And then?'

'Just smoked salmon. I'm not really hungry.'

'Oh *baby*!' Lee leaned towards her and covered her hand, an expression of concern puckering her immaculately made-up features. 'Wedding nerves, is it?'

'Well it's getting near.' Becky replied awkwardly.

'Darling,' Lee pressed her hand harder. 'That's really what I wanted to talk to you about.'

'The wedding?'

'Not really.' Lee bit on her grissini. 'It's just that we have great plans for Max, and Daddy very much wants him to go over to the States. I mean big plans, not just head of the UK operation but to succeed Daddy when he retires.'

'Golly.' Becky looked dumbfounded. 'And I thought he was going on the redundancy list.'

'Oh sweetie, is *that* why you were nervous?' Lee gave a tinkly laugh and, removing her hand, looked sideways at the newscaster.

'One never knows. You said no one was

173

indispensable.'

'I was teasing. But the thing is that it is important to get Max over to see Daddy, and spend some time in Madison Avenue and, well, I did wonder whether it would be possible to postpone the wedding.'

'Postpone the wedding!'

'Only a few months. You did originally plan a spring wedding didn't you? Well summer is an even lovelier time of year to have one. No worries about snow or ice or fog.' Lee gave a realistic shiver.

'Did you discuss this with Max?'

'No I wanted to sound you out first. Of course I told him that he was being groomed to succeed Daddy.'

'But he never told me!'

'Well maybe he wants to keep it as a surprise. You know what men are like.'

'So if I agree to a postponement he will go over to America for six months?'

'Exactly. Ted will stay on until we get back.'

'We? You're going too?'

'Well naturally.' Lee looked surprised. 'I shall be in overall control once Daddy retires.'

'Oh then it won't be Max?'

'Max will be Chairman and Chief Executive of the entire organisation worldwide. But I, of course, will remain as President fulfilling the vital role of family continuity. Daddy founded the business after all.'

'I'll have to think about it.' Becky sat back,

looking speculatively at Lee while the waiter took their orders. She thought that Lee's effervescence was overdone, as though she was trying hard, but not very successfully, to conceal her excitement about something. Was it the prospect of having Max to herself in the US for six whole months? And what would be the marriage expectations then?

'Maybe we could bring the wedding forward and go immediately afterwards? Make it a honeymoon trip?' She suggested without any apparent enthusiasm.

Lee frowned and shook her head. 'Not very business-like Becky. Besides Max would be so busy you'd be left out in the cold. You don't want to start off married life on the wrong foot do you, dear? I can see all sorts of problems arising which later on you might come to regret. Besides I'd *love* a summer wedding! Maybe I could be matron of honour? I was going to suggest it anyway. What do you think? Or is it impertinent of me to ask?'

Becky didn't reply. She felt suddenly choked, as though she were drowning and the waters were closing over her.

CHAPTER TEN

Christmas; the first Max and Becky had spent together, with her family. This time last year they were keen, involved, interested, partly in love but not yet engaged.

Becky thought that the happiest time of her relationship with Max had been the six months between Christmas and the formal engagement: the slow burgeoning of love, the first experience of lovemaking, the notion of a final, lifetime commitment.

But then somehow it had started to turn sour and now she was faced with the very real possibility that she was about to marry the wrong man.

Could it be that the right man was looking quizzically at her over the heads of the crowd assembled for an evening party in the Versey's drawing room? Henry, tall and commanding, for once elegantly dressed in black jacket and tie. She hardly ever saw him dressed formally, but when she did she thought how stunning he looked. Before, it had been an objective appraisal; now it seemed more subjective. There was no doubt that Henry had come to mean something much more to her in the last few months.

He smiled at Becky, who smiled back, raising her hand to give him a slight wave. Her happiness on seeing him come in had been tempered by the sight of the companion at his side—his dynamic, attractive, clever agent, Sue. She had seen him ask her mother and father, standing at the door to receive guests, whether it was all right to bring Sue. Of course it was. They'd nodded graciously, politely shaken hands and now he and Sue stood looking about them as though a little abashed by the company.

It was only proper for her to go and rescue them. She touched the arm of Max who was standing next to her talking animatedly to the mayoress.

'I must just go and have a word with Henry, darling. He looks a bit lost.'

Max looked up sharply.

'Oh? I'll come with you.'

'Really—'

'No,' The mayoress raised a hand protestingly, 'you two young people go off together. Don't let me detain you.'

'We'll be back in a second,' Max assured her. 'Becky just wants to see an old friend.'

They pushed through the assembled crowd. Some, who had not met Max, turned to try and delay them in greeting. Hands were pressed, promises made to return. Becky felt happy, excited, but she was also aware of a sense of alarm, a feeling of dread. The expression on Henry's face as he'd looked at Susan . . .

'Hi!' He lowered his head as she reached up to kiss his cheek.

'Hi!' she replied. 'So glad you could bring Susan.'

'We've some marvellous news,' Henry said, face glowing.

'Oh?' There was the lump in her throat, the faint, inexplicable, ridiculous feeling of nausea.

She looked at Susan, whose face also glowed. 'I'm so happy for you,' Becky said woodenly, turning to shake her hand.

'Happy for *me*?' She looked surprised. 'Happy for *Henry*!'

'Well of course happy for Henry. Happy for you both.'

She observed the mocking expression on Henry's face, the laughter in his eyes, the tender curve of his mouth.

'I don't think you quite understand,' he said, a suggestion of amusement lingering in his low, deep voice.

'What is there to understand?' Max joined in, hooking a proprietorial arm through Becky's.

'Henry has had his book accepted!' Susan's voice was shrill with excitement. 'What else?'

'Oh that is absolutely *wonderful* news!' Becky felt a wave of relief sweep through her. She flung her arms round Henry's neck. This time her mood was entirely different. He noticed it, sensed the pressure of her lips and, for a fraction of a second longer than necessary, left his cheek against hers.

'I only heard this morning,' Susan babbled on. 'I came straight down to tell him myself.'

'I'm over the moon with happiness.' Henry's eyes still looked steadfastly into Becky's. 'It's a life's ambition realised.'

'And a good publisher,' Susan said with enthusiasm. 'They love his book and want him

178

to do more.'

'What's it called?' Max's tone was polite, impersonal.

'"*A tale of the sea*",' Henry said. 'It's about the voyage of a lone sailor which is really a journey of self-discovery.'

'It's not what you call an *easy* read,' Susan said. 'It's a literary novel of great merit. I, and his publishers, think Henry has a great future.'

'Just what is all this?' Sir John, observing the excitement, approached the group, a drink in his hand. 'Somebody is very happy about something.'

Now it was Becky's turn to bubble over. 'Henry's had his novel accepted Daddy. It's going to be published. Isn't that thrilling?'

'That's great news Henry.' Sir John looked pleased. 'One day we shall say how proud we are to know you.'

'You can say that already Sir John,' Susan said. 'His publisher even thinks his novel may be a possible selection for the Booker prize. Imagine that, a first novel being selected for the Booker.'

'Hey steady on!' Henry gave a nervous laugh. 'I think you're jumping the gun a bit, Susan darling.'

Darling! Inwardly Becky bridled. Did he mean it, or was he already adopting the affectations of the literary world? Darling indeed! Soon there would be a round of parties, lunches, international congresses, appearances on TV. Henry would be lionised.

Inevitably he would change, become vain. Maybe he would even move away from Steethey.

At that moment she felt a stab of loss, almost of panic and, as she gazed desperately into Henry's eyes she could feel that he understood. But there was another slightly unfathomable, slightly defiant, expression too, and he slipped an arm through Susan's as though to show Becky that her change of heart had come too late.

But Sir John was clapping his hands, calling for silence and, gradually, people stopped talking and turned towards him as he leapt on a chair, his face wreathed in smiles.

'I want to make an announcement,' he cried, 'but first of all I want to welcome you all to our annual Christmas party, to say how good it is to see old faces, meet some new ones, and wish you all a happy Christmas and a prosperous New Year.'

There was a murmur of reciprocity as he turned to bring Max and Becky into the picture. 'It is with mingled sadness and joy that I announce that in a month's time my darling daughter, Rebecca, will become Mrs Max Lavery.' There was a fresh burst of applause as Max turned to Becky and kissed her softly on the mouth. 'I hope that as many of you as can will squeeze into the church,' Sir John went on, 'and, of course, you will all receive invitations to the reception which will be held here.' Once again there was applause and Sir John had difficulty calming his audience. 'Finally,' he said, then more loudly, 'finally, ladies and gentlemen, another piece of exceptionally good news has just been brought to my notice.' He pointed towards Henry. 'Henry Lamb, son of my old friend Tony Lamb, who has been almost a son to me too for many years, has had his first novel accepted.'

'Oh!' This time the reaction was immediate and genuine, and another storm of applause ensued while Henry, his dark, handsome face suffused with pleasure, stood gazing helplessly at the frenzied crowd, while with a swift, intimate gesture, Susan caressed his cheek with her fingers.

'As you know,' Sir John went on, 'Henry is a sailor, the son of a sailor, but as he has pressed on with his writing, enduring many rejections, he has shown all those qualities for which sailors are famous: hard work, tenacity and courage. It has been rewarded and we all wish Henry the best of luck in his career. But Henry ...' Sir John held out a finger in mock warning, 'don't forsake the sea!'

'There's no fear of that!' Henry shook his head amid laughter and, as Sir John jumped off the chair, the crowd pressed forward to shower congratulations on one of its favourite sons.

Max, gazing somewhat critically at the scene, murmured sotto voce: 'A very popular bloke, obviously.'

'It's because Henry's local,' Becky nodded. 'In a small community like this we all take people to our hearts and their joys and sorrows are our own.'

'And shall *I* ever be accepted as a son of the sea?' There was a note of sarcasm in Max's voice.

'Only if you live here,' Becky said lightly.

'You mean you still want your father to buy us that house up the hill, even though it's so unsuitable?'

'You haven't even seen it.'

'I have seen the particulars and it's falling to bits.'

'Daddy's had an architect look round it and he said that basically it's sound.'

'But, darling, I don't *want* to live out in the sticks.' He gestured contemptuously around. 'All these people; who are they? Nobodies!'

'Thank you very much.' Becky's tone was icy. 'These are people I've grown up with and love.'

'Oh come off it, Becky. You're the daughter of "Sir John", the local bigwig. Don't try and tell *me* that you're a daughter of the sea, the female counterpart of Henry Lamb. Any minute now you'll start having art exhibitions and become famous too.'

'Would you mind?' She gazed at him challengingly.

Max chuckled. 'I wouldn't mind but frankly, darling, I don't think it's likely. You have talent, sure, but not in that class. I don't think we're

182

likely to see one of *your* paintings at the Summer Exhibition.'

'Thank you for your faith in me!' Becky said bitterly and, turning on her heels, rapidly crossed the room before the tears stinging her eyes became visible.

She reached the door and ran out into the hall where, for a moment or two, she clung to the banister.

Suddenly a hand came down on her wrist and, with a gasp, she turned to see her mother's wise, kind eyes gazing anxiously down into hers.

'Darling. Becky? What is this? *Tears*, when you should be so happy.' She draped her arms round her daughter's shoulders and ushered her into Sir John's study which was the next door along. A soft light glowed from beside his desk as though he had been interrupted while working at it and, as the curtains remained undrawn, the beautiful expanse of moonlit sea gleamed like a field of diamonds. For a moment Becky's head rested against her mother's breast, her body shaken with sobs.

'Darling, darling, what *is* it?' Margaret Versey tried to tip up her chin and gaze into her eyes. 'Did you have a row with Max? I thought neither of you looked very happy tonight. Really darling . . .' there was a note of despair in Lady Versey's voice, 'it is a bit near to the wedding to be having rows.'

'It wasn't just *that*!' Becky made an effort to

control herself. 'He's always so nasty about Henry . . . and then about me.'

'You?' Lady Versey looked surprised.

'He said I fancied myself as an artist, but if I thought I'd get a picture into the Royal Academy I was wrong. Frankly I've been feeling a bit strung up, I know, but I did think that was the end.'

'Oh dear!' Her mother sat down and reaching for Becky's hand drew her down beside her. 'I guess Max is a bit unhappy too. You must understand that.'

'But why should Max be unhappy?' Becky took the handkerchief proffered by her mother and dried her eyes.

'He seems to think his job might be on the line at the agency.'

'Max?' Becky cried in astonishment. 'But he's being groomed for the succession!'

'Well . . .' her mother looked dubious. 'Is he? He's not too sure. He had a long talk with Daddy yesterday and expressed to him doubts that he was reluctant to put to you. He had to tell Daddy because of the question of putting money into the house. But he seems to feel that Lee may stay on here as head and he really doubts if he could work permanently as a subordinate to her.'

'Lee here?' Becky could scarcely believe her ears.

'That's the way it looks. Max would be number two. He's not keen on that. He feels he's been deceived but until it's all resolved he doesn't want to say anything.'

Lady Versey leaned towards her daughter and pressed her hand. 'Above all he doesn't want to say or do anything that upsets you darling just before the wedding. Obviously he wants it to go ahead. He loves you so much and depends on you too you know that. You couldn't possibly change your mind about him now, could you Becky? Not when he's feeling low and miserable, with his future at stake. You'd never forgive yourself if you did such a mean, contemptible thing.'

*　　　*　　　*

The wedding dress of thick cream velvet transformed Becky from a pretty, active, extrovert-looking girl who painted and liked messing about in boats, into something much more ethereal, a vision of loveliness, a medieval princess, a creature from a fairy tale. The high collar stood away from her neck and plunged into a deep V bodice which, in turn, flared into a full skirt down to her ankles. The long sleeves tapered down to her wrists.

Watching her daughter as she slowly pirouetted in front of the mirror, Margaret Versey had tears in her eyes. Becky's short golden hair was flung back and the profile presented by the delicate curve of her chin and her straight nose was exquisite.

As the bride-to-be slowly revolved, the seamstress pinned a tuck here, a length of the hem there.

'I don't think any *couture* could have been as good as that,' Lady Versey said after the seamstress once more stepped back for inspection.

'Neither do I.' Becky joined her fingers together in an attitude of prayer and, propping her chin on them, gazed gravely, critically at herself in the mirror. 'Yes I like it. Let's show Max.'

'Oh no!' Her mother's hand flew to her face in horror. 'It's unlucky!'

'Don't be silly Mummy,' Becky scoffed, 'This is the twentieth century.'

'It was the twentieth century when I was married,' her mother replied acidly, 'but this is an old legend, isn't it Grace?' She turned for confirmation to the dressmaker.

'Well...' Grace, not wishing to displease either of her clients, whose patronage she valued, looked helplessly from one to the other.

'It's only a superstition,' Becky said firmly, gathering up her skirts and making for the door. 'Pure superstition. Max is *dying* to see the dress.'

Max sat in the drawing room reading the paper, a cup of coffee by his side. As the door burst open and his bride entered he thrust the paper aside and rose eagerly from his chair.

'What . . .?' he began.

'Like it?'

'Darling it's wonderful.' He watched her as she spun several times round the room. 'But isn't it—'

'What?' She stopped and looked at him, her eyes smiling wickedly.

'Unlucky?'

'Oh, you don't believe that tosh?'

'Of course I don't.' As she stopped twirling he took her in his arms. 'You look so delectable, desirable . . .' His eyes wandered to the door.

'Not *here,*'she said mischievously. 'Especially not in my *wedding* dress!'

'Oh Becky!' His mouth was very close to hers. 'I really believe you are mine.'

'Of course I'm yours!'

Their mouths melted together and they remained for some moments locked in a deep embrace. As they broke apart Max murmured, 'Sometimes during this holiday I have asked myself if you were. I feel there's been a constraint between us.'

They released each other and Becky sat down opposite him, feeling incongruous now, slightly ridiculous in her wedding dress. Maybe it had been a rather silly, impulsive, mad idea, brought on by she didn't know what.

But at least it had given them a chance to talk, a chance that had eluded them during the hectic days of the holiday with the parties, the lunches, the dinners which citizens as prominent as the Verseys were expected either to attend or give. Small chance to talk when, finally, they had flopped into bed in the small hours and risen from a drugged sleep several hours later to be plunged in at the deep end all over again.

They had had no chance to talk at all. Or, perhaps, it had been an excuse to avoid it. Now her nails were pressing deep into the arms of her chair; although she knew it was against convention, she *had* wanted to confront Max in her wedding dress, just to see his reaction.

'It's a difficult time.' Becky gnawed at a finger. 'I'm also ...' she paused and studied the floor.

'Yes?' he prompted.

'I'm also very sorry, Max, that you chose to confide the truth about the agency in Daddy rather than me.'

'The *truth*?'

'About Lee.' She felt her anger, hitherto suppressed, welling up inside her.

'What truth about Lee?' His tone was peremptory.

'That she may be your overall boss.'

'Oh that!' Max looked immediately disconcerted.

'And that if she is you will probably leave. Why couldn't you tell *me* that Max? If you can't confide in me now, as I'm about to become your wife, when will you be able to?'

188

'Well!' Max, becoming annoyed, shook his head. 'I was hoping your father wouldn't say anything.' He rose abruptly and, hands in his pockets, a frown on his face, went over to the window, where he stood looking broodingly out at the sea. 'He betrayed a confidence in telling you.'

'He didn't tell me. Mummy did.'

'I see.' As he turned she could see how angry he was. 'And you kept this all the time to yourself? All this holiday without a word? No wonder you were unresponsive.'

'We've been so busy, so tired at nights, the chance never came up. Besides, if we had a row I thought it might spoil Christmas.'

'Maybe you're right.' He nodded and gave a wan smile. 'Well it *is* partly true.'

'Partly?' She looked surprised as Max flopped into the chair opposite her, crossing one leg over the other.

'You see, the house we've decided on in Marlow is, as you know, very expensive. Your father has offered to foot part of the bill and I had to tell him I didn't know for sure how secure my job was.'

'In the hope that he would foot it *all*?' Involuntarily Becky's lips curled with contempt.

'Now don't say it like *that*, darling.' Max looked uncomfortable, then, with an edge to his voice, 'Don't forget this house was forced on us because you were so sentimental about a

189

place half the price, but of the same standard, just because it had been repossessed!'

'This house was *not* forced on us, Max. You wanted it.'

'I don't want to live in Steethey.' A mulish look came into his eyes.

'We don't *have* to have a country house, especially if times are hard, and getting harder. Your flat is perfectly adequate and we can always come here for weekends.'

'I wanted us to have our own place, Becky. It looks good. Lee wants us to have it . . .'

'Yet it appears that you are now at loggerheads with Lee. News which, I must say, came as a considerable surprise to me.'

'Not at loggerheads.' He nervously uncrossed and recrossed his legs. 'That is a foolish thing to say.'

'Well it's the impression I got through Mummy.'

'It's a wrong impression then, and nothing is definite. It is just that Lee *may*, after all, stay. It all depends on the billings. I don't want to let myself into a long-term financial commitment I may not be able to sustain. That's all it was, darling.' He rose and, going over to her, knelt at her feet and took one of her hands and kissed it. 'Don't let's quarrel at this time, darling. Let's eliminate *all* misunderstandings between us. You look so lovely as a bride. I can't wait for the day.'

Her head sank on to his hand. 'I wish we

190

could.' She remembered her mother saying it was bad luck to let her bridegroom see her in her wedding dress. Perhaps it was. 'But if we're to trust in each other you must *always* confide in me. Daddy really gave Mummy the impression your job was on the line.'

'That came over a bit strong.' He laughed nervously. 'I just want to be careful and not begin our married life with a colossal debt.'

'But seriously, if Lee stayed on would you leave?'

'Possibly.' He thoughtfully screwed up his eyes. 'I'd have to see what the terms were.'

'But she's never actually *discussed* you leaving?'

'Oh no! She wants me to stay. Why else would she be so keen on making sure that we had a good, even luxurious, lifestyle?'

'I must say it beats me.' Becky shook her head in bewilderment. 'I thought maybe she was in love with you.'

'*Becky*!' Max threw out his arms. 'What a silly thing to say. Is that why you have been so upset? I thought I'd put your mind at rest about *that*?'

'I've never known really, Max,' Becky said in a small voice. 'I've always felt insecure ever since Lee appeared on the scene. She's always been the other woman; not just a sexual threat, but your boss as well. I don't think that I'll really feel secure until we're well and truly married.'

She looked into his eyes searching for the reassurance she so desperately needed.

After all, the hours were ticking by.

CHAPTER ELEVEN

'Happy New Year.'

'Happy New Year.' Henry, who had been deeply engaged in untangling some fishing tackle in the stern of his boat, looked up as she sat down beside him. 'Had a good party?'

'Yes.'

'You went up to London?'

She nodded again. 'What did you do?'

'Read and went to bed at about eleven.'

'No Susan?' She kept her tone light.

'No Susan.'

'Didn't you see the New Year in?'

He shook his head. 'Never do.'

'But it's going to be such a *happy* one for you.'

'And you?' He regarded her gravely. 'The wedding's only three weeks off isn't it?'

She nodded, her throat suddenly dry. 'It's awful.'

'It's what?' He looked at her, startled.

She corrected herself sharply. 'An awful responsibility. I mean the ceremony, the house, the whole business.' She suddenly put her head in her hands and, after a while, was aware of a comforting hand on her shoulder.

192

'There, there!' Henry murmured soothingly. 'It can't be that bad.'

She wanted to stay with him, to find shelter and consolation in that firm, masculine embrace. She wanted to stay there for ever. But she knew she couldn't, and wouldn't. Nor did she deserve to. Henry was too good for her— too straight, too strong. She began to see herself as a ditherer, a waverer, and despised herself for it. She wasn't sure who she really *did* love. First one, then the other. First Max was strong, then Henry. It was despicable. Maybe the best thing would be to go away, run off, disappear . . . put everything behind her and start again. But how? Where? She briefly leaned her head against Henry's rough woollen jersey.

'You're not very happy, are you Becky?'

She shook her head.

'Then *why* go ahead with it?'

'Too late to back out.'

'Better to back out than make a mistake.'

'I've got the wedding dress, everything.'

'People sometimes change their minds at the altar.'

'I couldn't. Think of the embarrassment, especially to Mummy and Daddy who would never forgive me. Besides . . .'

'Besides what?'

'I would break Max's heart, and things aren't going too well for him businesswise.'

'That's still no reason to *marry* him . . . if you

don't love him.'

She looked up and saw Henry's questioning eyes on her.

'I can't,' she said and, suddenly tossing her head back, attempted a smile. 'Come on, let's go sailing.'

'*Now?*'

'Now. If you've time?'

Henry cast a dubious eye at the clouds. 'I think a wind is going to get up.'

'We can always come back. Come on let's do it! After all, it may be for the last time.'

*   *   *

As they slipped into the Channel, the mainsail billowing before them, Becky felt a communion with the elements, the wind, the sea, such as she had seldom felt before. Her misery lifted as the craft sped through the water, while Henry at the tiller steered it expertly into the estuary, taking advantage of the wind. She sat in the prow, the jib sheet in her hand, leaning well back to balance the boat. Away from the shelter of the harbour the water was choppy but, oh, so exhilarating. A surge of joy swept through her and she knew that as long as she had the freedom of the sea, the ability to sail against the wind and keep her balance, all would be well.

Henry, observing the change in her, smiled and waved his hand.

'It shows,' he shouted.

'What?' she called back.

'You're relaxing. You feel better.'

'Much.'

As he nodded approvingly she leaned further out as the boat keeled over to port. The mainsail billowed out and Henry drew it in to a close-haul so as to get the maximum amount of wind without capsizing the boat. The sun shone, the spray-flecked water gleamed, and Becky felt at one with nature; with nature, and with Henry too.

What chance would she get to go sailing once she was married, sailing like this on the wide open sea? If there was a boat it would be some huge powerboat in keeping with Max's pretensions, probably plying up and down the Thames, full of cronies in the advertising business with boring wives who all drank too much.

The flecks on the waves grew more numerous, the wind blew more strongly, and Henry's expression became thoughtful.

'We should get back!' he shouted. 'I think we're in for a storm.'

'I *love* it,' Becky yelled, holding the jib sheet so hard that it bit into her hand. She leaned as far back as she could over the side of the boat, her feet caught fast in the straps.

Suddenly one of the powerboats she had been thinking about, appearing as if from nowhere, could be seen bearing down on them.

It also seemed that the driver, his vision obscured by the spray, hadn't seen them. Power always gave way to sail, but in this case it was an emergency.

'Ready to gybe!' Henry sprang up, his hand on the tiller, to turn the dinghy sharply around, away from the boat. Becky prepared to dash to the other side and, as Henry brought the tiller towards him, the wash from the boat, which missed them by a few inches, propelled the boom over catching Henry a blow on the side of the head which knocked him into the water. For a moment the boom swung wildly and, with a gasp of horror, Becky let go the jib sheet and rushed to take control of the tiller and bring the wildly swinging boom under control. To the starboard she could see Henry's head above the water rapidly receding as the dinghy, hastened by the fast current, continued its race towards home.

She let the jib flap, tightened the mainsail and brought the tiller hard down. Then, fixing Henry's position, she began the wide run for the routine man-overboard procedure. At first this appeared as though she was deserting the figure in the water, but once she had got a fair distance she hauled in the mainsail and, by skilful steering, brought the dinghy alongside the man in the water, who had fortunately been wearing a life jacket. As she reached Henry she could see that he was unconscious, was being rapidly carried out to sea with the tide, and leaning as far out of the boat as she could, half in, half out, she managed to catch hold of his lifejacket and with immense effort dragged him aboard. He lay with his head on the seat, his legs still dangling in the water. She seized the mainsail sheet, brought the tiller hard over and set a course for the shore.

At the same time she produced a flare from the stove in the locker and set it off in the hope that someone would see them from the shore and send out a faster boat. Henry's eyes were shut, his face grey, and there was a horrible purple mark at the base of his skull. But he was alive, she was sure of that.

However, sick with dread, she set off another flare and then another all the time continuing to use her skills as a yachtswoman to maintain the course for the shore.

Then her heart leapt. A powerboat, maybe the one that had nearly rammed them, appeared like a small speck from the estuary, growing larger and larger until, a few yards from them, it cut its engines and one of the two men on board threw her a rope. Becky, letting the sails flap, which almost brought the dinghy to a stop, seized it as one of the men hung over the side of his boat to grasp the dinghy with both hands.

'Is he alive?' he yelled.

'I think so. You'll have to get him straight to hospital.'

'We'll have to haul him aboard,' the other

man called cheerfully to his companion and with the boat now alongside the dinghy the pair of them, as carefully as they could, dragged, and lifted Henry's inert body into their boat.

'Will you be all right?' one yelled to Becky, who signalled frantically with her hands for them to get away. Then, as the engine roared into life, she sat back in the stern of the dinghy, gathered together the sheets of the mainsail and jib and, bringing the tiller towards her, set a course in the wake of the fast-disappearing powerboat. All at once she felt chilled to the bone, her hands and body freezing, her heart as cold as ice.

Supposing that by that impulsive, absurd but above all *selfish* idea to go sailing on a cold January day, she had helped to bring about the death of Henry?

She started to shake.

* * *

Her clothes still soaking, Becky tiptoed into the ward and stood by the side of the motionless figure in the bed. At his head a nurse was monitoring some gadget, and Becky gazed forlornly at the doctor by her side.

'He looks terrible!'

'He'll be okay. He's concussed. Nothing broken, no serious head injuries, as far as we can tell. We'll have to move him to Southampton when he is well enough, to do a

198

scan.'

'Shouldn't he be moved there now?' Becky asked anxiously.

Henry's eyelids flickered. He seemed to be trying to open his eyes, failed, gave a deep sigh and wriggled in the bed.

'See, he's okay.' The young doctor smiled with relief. 'All reflexes normal. I don't even think he'll need a scan, but we'll do one in a day or two just to be sure. He got a nasty ducking. How did it happen?'

'We had to do an emergency turn to get out of the way of a powerboat. The wash caught us, swung the boom over and knocked Henry into the water.'

'Nasty!' The doctor's tongue clicked sympathetically, but as a sailor himself he knew that she'd done a good job. 'You probably saved his life. In fact you *undoubtedly* saved his life.'

'The flares saved his life,' Becky said remorsefully. 'Thank *heaven* he had those on board. It took me so long to get into harbour he'd have died of hypothermia.'

'Sure you're all right?' The doctor gave her an appraising glance.

'Sure,' she said shivering. 'Just scared.'

'It must have been terrifying.'

'It was.' She shivered again.

'You should get out of those wet things.' The doctor looked at her with concern. 'You'll catch pneumonia.'

199

'I wanted to be sure Henry was recovering.'

'He's fine. You'll be the next if you're not careful. I'll ask Sister to get you some sort of robe. Out of those wet things and have a cup of tea with brandy. Instantly.'

'You're *sure* he'll be all right?' For a long moment Becky stood looking at Henry, and then on impulse she took the hand which lay limply on the white coverlet, and held it for a moment. Imperceptibly she felt him return the pressure.

'Is this the man you're engaged to?' The doctor indicated the ring on her finger.

'No, he's a friend.' Reluctantly Becky let his hand fall. 'A very old, *special* kind of friend.'

Then, remembering again what had nearly happened to him, she began to tremble and the doctor hustled her out of the ward to Sister's room across the corridor.

'Why, Miss Versey!' Sister said jumping up. Sir John was patron of the cottage hospital which had been founded by his wife's grandfather. 'You're soaking wet. Was it you in the boat with Henry?'

Between bouts of shaking Becky nodded.

'You must get out of those wet things.' Sister bustled around with motherly concern. 'I don't know what you were thinking about coming straight here. You should have gone home and changed.'

'She was worried about Mr Lamb.' The doctor was new to the hospital and hadn't known the people involved as intimately as Sister, who had been there for twenty years. 'I told her he'd be OK.'

'Henry just got a nasty case of concussion.' Sister's voice was disapproving. 'He should *never* have been out in this weather and with *you*, of all people!' Her expression was shocked. 'Engaged to be married! What will your fiancé say? Henry must have taken leave of his senses. It doesn't seem *at all* like him to take such a risk.'

'I insisted. I felt like it. He warned me against it and we were about to turn back; then we got into the wash of a powerboat which came too near. The boom heeled over, sending Henry into the sea. Otherwise we'd have been OK.'

'Lucky he wasn't drowned.' Sister's tone was still censorious. 'Now, Miss Versey, you get out of those clothes and into a nice warm robe. You'd better stay here overnight so that we can check on you.'

'I'm *absolutely* fine,' Becky began then, seeing the expression on Sister's face, said with an obedient smile, 'Oh alright, just in case, and thank you.'

* * *

'My precious darling.' She opened her eyes at the sound of Max's voice. 'That man must have been *crazy* to take you out to sea. You could

201

have drowned.'

'I was OK. *He* was nearly drowned.'

Max sat by the side of the bed, her hand in his.

'I came as soon as I could.'

The magnificent bunch of flowers beside her bed was from Lee. Her mother and father, Miles and his girlfriend Helen had come and gone. Mother twice.

She still felt cold and jumpy. They'd given her a shot. Said she was suffering from shock. As she gazed at Max the trembling continued. In her mind's eye she saw the boom swing over, knocking Henry into the sea. Her eyes filled with tears.

'It was,' she said between gulps, 'awful.'

'Of *course* it was awful. A dreadful experience. I can't think of anything worse. When Henry gets better I'll give him a piece of my mind. He took an awful risk.'

'Don't blame *Henry*. Blame me. I wanted to go out. I . . .' her tears brimmed over, 'I thought it might be the last time, you know.'

'What do you mean "the last time"?'

'Before we got married. I know you don't like sailing.'

'I certainly don't, and this proves me right.'

'Not if you go out in the right conditions. We took a risk.'

'You stick to dry land my girl, in future; walking the dog or some such.'

'You really mean that don't you?'

202

'Yes I do.' Max's clasp tightened. 'I'm never, ever going to let you go to sea again. You're far, far too precious for me to lose.'

She closed her eyes. The shaking had stopped. Instead she felt terribly drowsy, numbed. She could hardly feel the tips of her fingers or toes. She saw the dinghy on the calm, even surface of the sea, the sails billowing in the gentle breeze, as they sailed into the sunlight.

A smile illuminated her face as she drifted gently into sleep.

*   *   *

Much later when Becky woke, only a lamp on a table burned dimly in the private room. She felt warm, at peace, happy. It must have been the effects of the drugs, but already she felt better. The pungent smell of many flowers filled the room. She thought they took them away at night, but maybe the nursing staff had forgotten. She was glad they had.

She looked at her watch. It was eleven. Very peaceful and calm in the small twelve-bed hospital. She had been born here and in a way it was almost like home.

She crept out of bed and for a moment sat on the side to steady herself. She put her feet out to feel her slippers. They were warm, the robe was warm. She still felt drowsy, but deliciously at peace.

She went into the bathroom, brushed her teeth and gazed at her face in the mirror. She looked very pale, interesting almost. She let herself out into the corridor, paused and listened. Nothing stirred. There were no sounds of people crying out in pain, no lusty cries of new-born babies.

Becky tiptoed to the end of the corridor and gently turned a doorknob, looking inside. Henry slept on his back, his eyes closed, illuminated as she had been, by the dim light of a lamp in the corner of the room. His face looked beautiful, serene, peaceful; there was a day's growth of dark beard on his face, a shock of black hair on his pillow. He was breathing evenly and peacefully. He was OK. She sighed deeply with a feeling of thanksgiving.

As quietly as she could she drew up a chair and sat by his side taking his hand in hers. Immediately his fingers tightened around hers and, his eyes opening, he focused them unsteadily on her.

'I nearly killed you,' he said.

'You nearly killed yourself,' she replied in a low voice. '*You* were the one who went into the water.'

'We should never have gone. I was mad.'

'I insisted. It wasn't your fault.'

'It *was* my fault.' His voice dropped to a whisper. 'I wanted to be alone with you. You said it might be the last time ... I love you Becky. Always have, always will.'

204

She squeezed his hand and, with a deep sigh, rested her head against it, too weary, too confused, too miserable to attempt to reply.

CHAPTER TWELVE

Lee, with swathes of material over her arm, samples of wallpaper in her hand, followed by a harassed assistant making notes, could indeed have been the owner, rather than a somewhat bemused Becky, who trailed behind the assistant trying hard to take in what was being said.

The house was long, low, gracious, overlooking the Thames. Its velvety lawn ran down to the river, a central, ornamental fountain now silent. At the back were garages, stables, and a drive half a mile long which joined the main London road. It was indeed, as Max had said, very like the house Becky refused to live in only it was almost twice the price, its previous owners, wealthy Americans, having recently moved out to return to the States, well pleased with having got their asking price. Contracts had been signed, but completion had not yet taken place. By permission of the vendors they were being allowed to inspect the house.

Very little, in fact, needed doing. The house could have been moved straight into; but, of course, places never were as the purchaser wanted. Or, to be more truthful, not quite as Lee wanted.

The fact that Lee was not the actual purchaser did not deter her at all.

'I think if we knock *this* wall down ...' a richly bejewelled hand gestured in front of her, 'we can then have a long, low room with that beautiful view of the river.' She turned as though realising, for the first time, who exactly was behind her. 'What do you think, Becky?'

'I think it's fine.' Becky stared at the view of the river and thought of Steethey and the incomparable sight of the sea.

'You don't seem very interested Becky.' Lee gazed at her sharply. 'It is, after all, to be *your* home.'

'Oh but I *am*.' Becky guiltily switched her mind from a contemplation of the sight of Steethey Bay from her bedroom window, to that of the flat waters of the Thames in front of what was to be her new home.

'And I think the William Morris here,' Lee continued, holding a swatch of drapery up against the wall, 'with matching curtains and pelmets. Do you agree Becky?'

Again Becky nodded vigorously while the assistant scribbled notes.

And so on and so forth throughout the house; the drawing room which, with a wall knocked down, would stretch from one side to the other, the dining room, a smaller room which would be an informal sitting room, probably with a TV, a room next to that which would be Max's study, a lavatory and washroom, a breakfast room, an enormous kitchen with two utility rooms and then up the wide staircase to a hall, off which were the master bedroom suite and four guest bedrooms, all similarly en suite. There was a second floor with six smaller bedrooms, two bathrooms and a suite which could obviously be turned into a nursery. They spent little time up here, Lee either thinking that the advent of a family would be delayed, or feeling—as Becky was—knocked off her feet. It had been a long, hard, busy day.

Yet in the empty house there was no chair to sink into and instead Lee sat on the still carpeted floor of the living room, her arms round her knees. By now her assistant had been dispensed with and had stumbled out clutching her pad crammed with notes, the swatches of materials, samples of wallpaper, clearly on the verge of exhaustion.

'It's terribly good of you to do all this.' Becky squatted down beside Lee, with some difficulty in her pencil slim skirt which threatened to give at the seams.

'But I'm delighted . . .' Lee stifled a yawn, 'if a little surprised that you *allowed* me to do it.'

Becky gazed at her in astonishment.

'But you *wanted* to! In fact I thought you insisted. Max said you had such good taste.' She tried to keep the irony out of her voice.

'But you're the artist, after all,' Lee continued as if she hadn't heard. 'I would have thought you'd have started on doing up this place as soon as contracts were signed.'

What Lee didn't add was that she herself could never stop interfering, however hard she tried. She was the sort of person who made everyone else's business her own.

'I've quite a lot to do thank you,' Becky riposted tartly, 'preparing for the wedding. There are only so many hours in the day.'

'Don't I know it.' Lee jumped up, consulting her neat Cartier watch. Then she produced her mobile phone from her briefcase and dialled a number before putting it to her ear.

Becky watched with the awed fascination that Lee always seemed to induce in her as she made a note of the messages, several requests and, finally, an item of news which seemed to please her, for as she put the phone back in her case she had a smug look on her face.

'We've secured the agency in Italy. Thanks to Max,' she informed Becky with a smile. Max had flown to Milan two days before.

'That's terrific news.' Becky leaned back against the wall. 'What a relief.'

'A relief?' Lee looked surprised. 'Not exactly that. After all we expected it.'

'Oh?'

'Why should you say it was a relief?' Lee pressed on, 'I don't quite understand.'

'Well . . .' Becky carefully examined her

208

nails, 'I thought things weren't too good?' She raised her eyes to gaze at Lee.

'Not too *good*? They're excellent. Very good indeed. We have a share of the market in all the major European capitals as well as New York and London.'

Slowly Becky rose and fastened the buttons of her Courrèges suit. 'Why, then, did you sack half the art department?'

'We have to slim down in certain key areas,' Lee replied briskly. 'A lot of the copy goes straight to animation and we don't need artists; the animators do it on the computer. Besides, there are plenty of talented freelance artists on the market like you, and we hope to make more use of them. Supasoop are anxious to extend their range and begin a new campaign, and asked for *you* specifically.'

Becky didn't appear impressed.

'Then Max's job *isn't* on the line?' Her eyes finally focused on Lee.

'Max?' Lee looked startled. 'Of *course* Max's job isn't on the line. Whoever said it was?'

'Max did.'

'He must have been kidding you.'

'Why should he?'

'That is . . .' Lee appeared to be thinking rapidly, 'unless he's thinking of leaving. I certainly hope he isn't. My God, all the work I've done on that man.'

'He is still being groomed to succeed Ted Levine?'

'Of course! Ted has virtually left. All that remains to be settled are the terms of his redundancy. I certainly hope he's not going to scupper the works. Daddy would be furious.' An unpleasant frown darkened Lee's brow.

'Maybe Max got the wrong end of the stick?' Becky suggested.

'I don't see why. It's always been perfectly plain; perfectly straightforward.'

'And you're definitely going back to the States?'

'Of course. Have to.' She gave Becky a typically arch smile and continued. 'Someone's waiting for me there. As a matter of fact I may be following in your footsteps in the summer.' Now she looked positively coy.

'You mean *marriage*?' Becky gasped.

Lee nodded, her face transformed by a soft, feminine smile of the kind that Becky could never recall having seen on her face before. 'An awfully *nice* guy, a banker. He's divorced too. He asked me this Christmas. We've been dating a couple of years. Maybe that's why I've taken you two lovebirds to my heart. I've kinda taken a tumble too.'

'Oh, I'm so thrilled for you!' Spontaneously Becky rushed up to her and hugged her.

Was it that she was relieved too? That the threat of a romance between Max and Lee had been lifted once and for all? Did her heart flood with joy because now she and Max could marry without the shadow of Lee hanging over them? Was *this* why she had been afraid of Lee all along? Was it this that had affected her feelings for Max?

'Why thank you.' Lee seemed touched by the gesture. 'But you have worried me Becky. Max is *so* talented, so *good* at his job. I do hope he hasn't been head-hunted by someone else? You've put a fear in my heart now.'

'Oh I don't think so.' Becky was anxious to reassure her. 'Maybe it was just a rumour that went around the agency because of the redundancies in the art department and . . .' she hesitated, not wishing to discuss matters of personal finance with Lee. But Lee clearly expected her to continue. 'Well actually there *is* something else. My father offered to put up some money for a house for us; not entirely, you know, but to help.'

'I understand.' Lee nodded encouragingly.

'Max told Daddy that the job outlook was doubtful, and he thought he couldn't afford to take on a large mortgage. He told me that too, that he didn't want to go into marriage saddled with debt. I didn't particularly want a large house, but Max insisted.'

'Quite right.' Lee nodded approvingly. 'Most important to keep up appearances. It impresses clients.'

'So . . .' Becky looked round, 'the whole of this house is being paid for by Daddy.'

To her surprise Lee clapped her hands together, threw back her head and gave a delighted laugh.

'Oh what a *clever* man your Max is! That is perfectly splendid. You think we'd get rid of a good businessman like that? Oh no, never in a thousand years!'

A little block of ice seemed to lodge itself inside Becky's heart.

'I beg your pardon? I don't think I understand.'

'My dear . . .' Lee impulsively clasped her shoulder. 'Max is just applying to his private life good business principles. He knows your father can afford the house. I believe he's a millionaire, incidentally. Max doesn't know what the future holds and is right not to wish to go into marriage burdened by personal debt.'

'But how does he know my father can afford it? He has many commitments.' Becky felt a furious blush rise to her cheeks.

'Oh come on ducky,' Lee scoffed, 'your old man is rolling.'

'Then Max is taking Daddy for a ride?'

'Not at all. Just being rather clever, I'd say. Don't worry, your daddy can afford it—he wouldn't do it if he couldn't—and *I'd* say that by the time all the alterations have been done and the place has been redecorated he won't grudge a penny. Come on now . . .' she companionably linked an arm through Becky's, turning off the light as they walked towards the door, 'let me take you somewhere nice for dinner. Isn't it all so *exciting*?'

*   *   *

They'd chosen a restaurant off the beaten track, out of town, where they were practically certain to see no one they knew. They drove there separately but arrived within ten minutes of each other. They sat in the bar outside the restaurant having drinks and studying the menu. The conversation was impersonal, rather stilted, awkward. Max could sense that Lee had something on her mind and he felt uneasy, even apprehensive. Lee certainly wasn't herself; not the calm, detached, aloof Lee he knew.

He'd arrived back from Italy with a new contract which he'd reported on at a meeting the previous day. Lee had taken the chair but left immediately afterwards without stopping to talk to him. Later when he returned to his office there was a message on his screen to call her, which he did on the internal phone. Briefly she'd suggested dinner and then, sensing his hesitation, said quickly, not at her place, and named a few restaurants out of town. After some discussion they agreed on the place where they were now.

They talked about Italy, the prospect of opening an office in Milan. Briefly Lee mentioned the house and her visit there with Becky.

They finished drinks and moved into the dining room which was dimly lit, full of well-dressed, well-heeled couples, maybe with a secret like their own. Instinctively Lee glanced round, but then she realised it wouldn't matter one bit if they did see someone they knew. Now they no longer had something to hide.

Their first course was on the table. The waiter, after seeing them into their seats and unfolding their napkins on their laps, poured the carefully selected wine, a beautiful greeny-golden vintage Meursault.

'I guess you wondered what's up?' Lee gazed at Max, her fingers playing nervously with the stem of the wine glass. Now she looked poised, elegant, calm. Her make up was discreet, her hair in the familiar upsweep of the ebony chignon. She wore a military style black trouser suit with black beading on the bodice, dressy but not too dressy.

'Well . . .' Max averted his eyes and gazed at the cloth.

'I give up, Max,' she said so quietly it was almost a whisper. 'I know I've lost. The thing is that I don't want to lose you, either as a friend or for the business. Personally I realise our relationship is at an end, but there is no need at all for you to consider leaving the firm.'

'How do you know?' Max raised his eyes.

'Becky told me you were worried about redundancy. I knew this wasn't true. This was a bluff. If you were talking of leaving there must be some other reason. I think I can guess what that is, but I wish you'd tell me the truth, Max, and I can see if there is something I can do about it.'

'I just think the situation between us is so difficult. Frankly it's impossible.' Max averted his eyes again and started to toy with his fork on the snowy white cloth. 'We can never go back to being as we were. You never told me you were going to stay on here as my overall boss. I understood you were going back to the States and, that not being being the case, I think the situation will be untenable.'

'So that is what you're worried about?'

'Yes.'

Lee leaned back in her chair, seemed visibly to relax. 'Then I can put your mind at rest. There's a guy back home in the States. I've known him for a while but, somehow, he didn't seem to measure up to you. On the plane going back for Christmas I realised that you and Becky were going through with the wedding and I had to give you up completely. Get over you for good.' She shrugged. 'It was hard for me to admit defeat, but there you are. Some you win, some you lose. This chap, his name's Joe, met me at the airport—roses, the lot. I guess I just threw myself into his arms. Didn't love him the way I loved you, but I wasn't going to continue to throw myself at someone who didn't want me. Stupid. I behaved like a schoolgirl . . . I had to get back my self-respect.'

'Please Lee . . .' Max, observing that she was close to tears, put his hand over hers. 'I never

215

thought of you in that way. I felt as much for you as you did for me. Okay,' he acknowledged, 'it wasn't love, maybe, but it was great tenderness, affection and respect. And I respect very much what you're saying now and what you're doing. I'm delighted if you have found a partner you feel you might be happy with and I wish you all the joy in the world. I'm sure we can continue to be friends and workmates and if you're going back to the States then the situation resolves itself.' He gave a deep sigh of relief and threw his hands expressively in the air. 'We can both make a new start.'

Lee put her glass to her mouth and, pausing, looked at Max. 'Do reassure Becky won't you? I think she's afraid you were going to be hard up with all this talk of redundancy. Getting her father to pay for the house was a shrewd move.'

Max felt the blood drain from his face. He stared, aghast, at this woman, who seemed determined to torment him one way or another. Now he saw all this as a manoeuvre, part of an elaborate trick, another sly strategem. He should have guessed that nothing, nothing about Lee Wylde was good or noble.

'You discussed *that* with Becky?'

Lee looked, or tried to look, all innocence. 'Why yes. She said you were so afraid of losing your job you felt you couldn't afford to take on a large mortgage.' Lee closed one eye and gave him a broad, conspiratorial wink. 'Nice one Max. You're a great businessman and I sure am proud to have you in the firm. What is more important, Daddy would be proud of you too.'

Max closed his eyes, his head swam. Once again he knew that Lee, however innocent she might pretend to be, was not innocent at all.

Once again, Lee had won.

*   *   *

The organ crashed out the opening bars of the Wedding March and the bride hung nervously on to her father's arm at the door of the church. The spectators who had gathered outside broke through the barrier to watch the couple as they prepared for that momentous walk to the altar. The local bobby had had to send for reinforcements and representatives of neighbouring constabularies were there in force.

An usher, however, firmly shut the door in the faces of the hopefuls as Becky and her father, after exchanging glances, began the slow, measured walk up the aisle. Behind them was Lee as matron of honour and six small relatives of bride and groom who carried the bride's train.

Ahead of her she saw Max rise from his pew and take his place to the right of the altar with his best man, Peter Merridin, both a colleague and an old schoolfriend. At the foot of the sanctuary stood the vicar, the prayer book between his hands, a beneficent smile on his face.

The solemn, glorious bars of the Mendelssohn Wedding March continued and, as Max turned finally to face his bride, her eyes squarely met his.

Here was a man, she thought, who had wooed and won her, captured her by the force of his personality, his undoubted success, his ambition, his dynamism; not least of all his good looks. He was a forceful, powerful man, the kind a woman dreamed of. The kind she had dreamed of ever since adolescence.

He was a man she had loved, whom she had allowed willingly to seduce her. She had given herself to him body and soul.

Yet he was also the man who had raped her, forced her to make love against her will.

He had lied to her, lied to her father, deceived him into spending much more money than he could probably afford. Millionaire he might be; but much of his money went back to his business.

Max had deceived her too, probably intentionally, into thinking he might be in love with another woman, Lee who had insisted on being matron of honour. With his encouragement she had patronised her, demeaned her, even while she pretended to be her friend. Probably behind Becky's back she had laughed at her too.

She had taken her over; dressed her, flattered her, decided on the redecoration of her house. How foolish could one woman make another feel?

Yet Max, her fiancé, had fawned on this same woman and allowed himself to be patronised, goaded, cajoled against his will by her too.

Max was also a man who had tried to denigrate his fiancée, making her unsure of her talent, uncertain of herself. He had mocked her friends, belittled them, especially one whom she held very dear.

It was obvious that he despised her family, took advantage of them, was out for what he could get and that, once married, she would be a mere chattel in his hands.

Why, oh why, had it taken her so long to see this? Why until she reached the very steps of the altar hadn't she realised what Max really was? This was the man who, forsaking all others, she was about to marry, give up the home she loved, the family she adored, the place she was happy in.

For him she would abandon one lifestyle in order to embrace another she found wholly inappropriate and artificial.

The music slowly tailed off, her father handed her to Max who reached for her, smiling. The best man stood next to him and produced the velvet box in which was the wedding ring. The vicar opened his prayer

219

book and peering at them through his golden pince-nez said, 'Do you think we should do the March again? I thought it a little too quick.' He raised his eyes to the organ loft as if for confirmation; the children gathered about the bride giggled and the tension of the moment seemed to snap.

Becky gazed at her mother, father, at Max's mother and sisters over from Australia, at Miles and his girlfriend, at Lee, the children, at the vicar, Peter Merridin and, finally, at Max, who was looking quizzically at her. She looked around at the empty church which in two days' time would be filled, with not a seat to spare. Outside the bunting was already going up in the streets for the wedding of the year. Steethey's favoured and, maybe, most favourite daughter. At Steethey House the caterers had already begun their elaborate preparations.

At the back of the church stood the ushers, a cleaner and the women whose job it was to do the flowers, so many that they had already begun. There would be great vases of chrysanthemum and Arum lilies, and orange blossom would hang from the stalls, the lectern, the pulpit and the choir.

She turned her eyes on the vicar who, as if to himself, had been running through the words of the service, waiting for the organist to consult with the choir and make up his mind. 'Then I shall say Rebecca Dorothy Versey, do you take this man—'

220

'*No!*' Becky shouted in a voice so loud that the sound reverberated violently round the church. 'No, no, no.'

Then, her eyes on the door, she began to run towards it, heedless of the hands stretched out to try and stop her, the gasps of horror that accompanied her, the plea of her mother crying in a loud voice, '*Becky!*'

The ushers jumped towards the door as she approached it, opening it just in time. Outside, the crowd who had come for the rehearsal surged forward, stopping only when they saw she was alone. Momentarily she paused on the steps staring at them as they, uncomprehending, stared back.

Then, suddenly, she dived through them, parting them with her arms.

She ran all along the village street, scattering astonished passers-by as she went. She leapt over the harbour wall, and ran along the path by the estuary, past the boats anchored in the bay.

She came to Henry's cottage and, her heart thudding, raced up the steps. She seized the handle, but the door was locked. She pounded upon it with her fists and, after what seemed an eternity, it opened and the man she really loved, the man she really wanted, stood, his pipe in his mouth, a book in his hand, gaping at her.

'What? Why, Becky!'

'May I come in?' she asked breathlessly.

221

'Of course!' Normality seemed to return as he stepped aside and she paused, breathing in the atmosphere of the room: the fire in the grate, books on the shelves, the lamplight glowing in the window, a pot of tea on the table. Sandy asleep on the hearthrug. She sighed and closed her eyes, exhaling loudly with happiness.

'Have you had tea?' Henry asked prosaically as he placed his book and pipe carefully on the table and, taking the lid off the pot, casually examined the contents.

'Tea!' she said. 'How delightful.'

'You seem very pleased about something?' His expression was of bewilderment.

She wanted to crush him in her arms, cover his face with kisses. But these emotions she managed, for the moment, to keep under control.

He disappeared abruptly into the kitchen and, even though he was gone only a short time, it was agony to wait until she saw him again.

Henry, Henry, I love you so much. How could I *ever* have thought ... why didn't I realise? She saw the boom swing over and pitch him into the water. That moment she knew how much she loved him, what his loss would mean to her. He could have been killed outright. People sometimes were. He could have been drowned in the turbulent sea and never found again.

He returned with the kettle and a mug which he put on the table, filling the teapot with hot water. Still looking puzzled, he replaced the lid and returned to the kitchen.

Oh he was lovely ... his dark face was so vital, his blue eyes so startling, his shock of black hair so sexy, his build so magnificent. How could she *ever* have preferred someone like Max to Henry?

Henry, Henry, I love you so much. How could I *ever* have thought ... oh, supposing you no longer love me ...

Her expression was crestfallen as he appeared and began to pour tea into the mug.

'How was the rehearsal?' he asked almost casually. 'Did it go well?'

'Very well.' She wanted to reach for his hand and kiss it.

'That's good.' He swallowed and glanced at the clock on the wall. 'It didn't take long.'

'Long enough ...' her face glowed with excitement, the doubt had gone. She went up to him so that their mouths almost touched, her eyes shining into his. 'Long enough for me to know you're the man I want, Henry. Henry will you marry me?'

She put her arms round his neck and he gazed at her, dumbfounded.

'Have you taken leave of your senses Becky?'

'Yes. I have taken leave of my senses. I do not want to marry Max Lavery. In fact I don't even like him. I . . .' A puzzled expression appeared on her face. 'In fact I think I can even say I *hate* him. I don't know why I *ever* got engaged to him when there was you, always *you* Henry.'

And then she allowed him to take her in his arms and, for the very first time, he kissed her full on the mouth.

*   *   *

The house was at the top of the hill with a fine view of the bay. They'd got it at about the right price, or rather Sir John Versey did.

There was quite a lot of talk in the village, scandal might be a better word, over the events that took place on that cold day in January when Becky Versey had deserted her bridegroom almost at the altar and declared her love for a man she had known all her life.

Max, hurt and humiliated, had been driven back to London by Lee who almost felt *she* had lost a bride too. Such had been the extent of her interference that Max blamed her for everything and abruptly quit his job at the agency. Eventually he went to Australia where his mother and two of his sisters lived and where he was to do extraordinarily well.

Once they had got over the shock Sir John and Lady Versey grew used to the idea of their daughter exchanging one fiancé for another in, well, it seemed almost a matter of hours.

Maybe a little of Becky's growing discontent with Max had passed on to them and Max's grasping and—as it proved—untruthful, behaviour over the house had not impressed Sir John at all. But by that time it had all seemed too late, and Becky's impulsive, and by some much criticised, conduct had proved a blessing.

As it was he was able to avoid completing the deal on the Thames valley house and although this cost him something, it also saved him a lot of money.

Becky and Henry were married very quietly in London at a register office early in the spring and went to Italy for a honeymoon. They liked it so much that they rented a cottage and while Becky painted the Tuscan sunsets to her heart's content Henry began a new novel.

They were free, they were young, terribly in love and could do as they pleased. Above all they could be *themselves*—well Henry had never been anything else—and Becky's costly *couture* collection eventually appeared in the Oxfam nearly-new shop to the joy of many local people.

And when they got back to Steethey the house was waiting for them. The house on the hill overlooking the bay which they both loved, in the place where they were both born and where, in fullness of time and, hopefully, after a long, happy life and lots of children, their bones would be laid peacefully to rest.